The Lost Scraps of Love

....that I found again...!!!

The Lost Scraps of Love

....that I found again...!!!

Nipun Ranjan

Srishti
PUBLISHERS & DISTRIBUTORS

SRISHTI PUBLISHERS & DISTRIBUTORS
N-16, C. R. Park
New Delhi 110 019
srishtipublishers@gmail.com

First published by Srishti Publishers & Distributors in 2010

3rd impression, 2011

Typeset in AGaramond 11pt. by Suresh Kumar Sharma at Srishti

Printed and bound in India

Prologue

Before you start the book why don't you answer three simple questions. And don't be afraid it's nothing related to science, maths or GK. It's related to just you and your choice, how you carry your life.

1. How much do you love your love?

(a) More than life

(b) Love them yes, but less than my self-dignity

(c) Love them alright, but less than my friends

2. How much do you love your friends?

(a) More than life

(b) Love them alright, but less than my self-dignity

(c) Love them yes, but less than my girlfriend and personal matters

3. What if your lover leaves you forever? What would you do?

(a) Keep trying for her/him hoping they will come back.

(b) Love her/him silently buː don't do anything, maybe wait for her forever.

(c) Forget her/him and continue with life, maybe with someone else who would be more loving.

Now whatever you answered just keep in mind while reading the book and be firm at whatever you chose. What were takes to these questions? Go on reading you'll find it out soon.

I was in my hometown as I had a week long holiday. I was sitting over the terrace of a temple with my best friend for seven years, Raj. This temple was least visited by people as it was in the deep interior of a colony. There were no stairs to climb up to the terrace, which made it the safest place for smoking even near my house in my hometown. We somehow managed climbing up with the help of broken walls.

It was 7:30 in the evening. The sky was dark and cloudy. This was the place where we used to sit and chat for hours and hours, share our secrets and discuss several of our problems as best friends do, Raj knew me better than my parents or any one else in this world except my girlfriend, rather ex-girlfriend with whom I had crashed our one-year old relation last month.

I don't know how it happened. It all started with such small things which I don't even remember and slowly it turned into such a catastrophe. The problem with misunderstandings is that when it adds up it mounts exponentially and finally leads to the end - to a point where she didn't want to talk to me or see me anymore. Neither did she pick up my calls nor did she reply to my SMSes. I mailed her but never got her reply. I tried scrapping her but she ignored me on Orkut also. I tried meeting her but she avoided me and I didn't want to create a scene or ruin her or my image. I couldn't do anything and was down in the dumps and was lying quiet with the 4th cigarette of the day in my hand.

"You're still depressed? It's been a month now. Forget that girl." Raj said sensing my melancholy. We two understood each other so well that in the school there was rumour of us being in gay relationship. But we didn't care and took it lightly.

"Forget her? It's not possible yaar. I still love her like mads" I replied in a choked voice. My problem is that I generally don't get attached to people easily and once I do I get addicted to them. I can't live without them.

"But she doesn't love you anymore. Why carry a one sided love? By the way, do u still remember Abhilasha? You wrote love letters and that friendship band and the money you stole from Sanjay bhaiya's wallet to buy her chocolates and greeting cards. Where is she now?" Raj said to make me deviate from my topic. He always used this trick to distract me but this time I didn't get trapped

"It's nothing like Abhilasha's case, she was just a crush. You don't know the depth of my relation. We met daily and spent hours and hours together for one long year."

"Aah again? You won't listen to me until I listen to you. Go"

"You know whenever I called her, I always got her number busy; the reason being she also called me at that very moment. When I SMSed her I got her SMS before I got the delivery report of my SMS, as if we pressed the keys together. Our likes and dislikes were also exceptionally similar. We made the best pair of which people gave examples. We had such a good understanding of each other. We agreed over everything. But in the last three months things got really changed..." I was muttering non-stop.

"Okay I got it all. Stop now. What do you want?" Raj put a brake on me.

"I want her. Whatever it takes." I said lighting up the fifth cigarette. I knew, I was breaking the promise I made to her-that I'd never smoke, and if I smoked it would not be more than one cigarette and I would tell her about it. Her promises were always full of clauses. I kept the promise till the end but what did promise stand for when she was not there? And think of her. How many promises did she break? The promise to be with me forever. The promise to marry me, to have kids. We had even decided the name of the kids."

"You will have to pay the price; it was your mistake afterall." Raj taunted.

"No it was not my fault, it was 50-50. Half the fault was mine and half hers"

"100 percent your fault. I know her. She is a Virgo and these people are very cool and soft hearted, but when they get angry with someone they can be horrible."

"Okay 80 percent, but I won't take more than that. You are taking her side? You are my friend or her?" I said being petulant.

"See how you are behaving; like a kid. Grow up man"

"Let me think what we can do here." He started musing and said "Don't u have any common friend?" Raj said closing his eyes and rubbing his forehead.

"No I broke contact with all her friends the day we broke up. I deleted all her friends from Orkut and ignored them"

"There you go. You think after you do and you never think of consequences, do you? You spoilt arrogant brat. That's the reason you are in this situation"

"May be. But how could she forget all the time we spent together?"

"Maybe she hasn't. Girls just don't show"

"But if she recalls all past moment, she would surely regret. She'd surely miss me"

"Idea here! Why don't you remind her of all your past times, time you spend together?"

"But how is that possible?" I said in reflex.

"Common friends could've been excellent option but since you have closed this way you will have to try extra hard, do something exceptionally innovative."

"Like what?"

"Like...aaa....You can write a book. In that book you can write about the things that might remind her" He said casually.

"Are you nuts? I can't do that." I said panicking. Someone was saying me to do the impossible.

"You said you can do anything to get her back, whatever it takes..Huh?" Raj caught me with my own words. He would make a very good advocate, I thought.

"But how is that possible? I can't even write a single page properly. How will I write a full book? And how will I get ideas?"

"You can simply start with the things you remember about her. And you have your and her e-mails and SMSes. I mean those romantic ones. And then you have her scraps on Orkut. The early ones, the romantic ones, the last ones – all the scraps. Start with those"

"You are driving me crazy. Bad idea. It's simply not possible. How will I manage time for writing? You know, it asks for hundreds of hours. And we have regular class tests and lab reports and semester"

"Don't make excuses. And don't tell me you don't have time. You do Orkutting all the day; I always find your green bulb glowing on Gtalk. And you don't have time?" Mr Lawyer broke any and all defences I made.

"What if it didn't work? I mean, if the book flops or if I couldn't get a publisher in the first place. Or if it gets published but she doesn't read the book. Or worse she gets angry with me for writing these and including her SMS, emails and scraps in the book?"

"Don't think like a pessimist. I trust you. Your aim is just getting her. Write your heart into it. Everything will go alright. Amen." He took a breathing break and continued "And why won't she read your book. She would definitely do. And God forbid, even if she doesn't read it, think this way. Mumtaz never saw Taj Mahal but world sees it. Getting what I'm saying? Most of the love stories get forgotten. Atleast you can make your love story immortal."

"Hmm" I nodded like a five year old being asked to lift fifty Kg. He always said these weird things which didn't have any meaning but somehow seem amusing.

"In this mean time don't try anything rubbish even if you see her in college. Let her miss you too. Gift her book straightway. And give her time to digest and excrete her anger and become cool again" Raj said

I was still in doubt whether I could complete the whole task. Was I choosing a wrong way? Should I try something else?

Operation Dog

In the last month I called her almost every hour of the day. SMSed her different versions of I'm sorry many a times. But neither my calls were picked, nor my SMSes were replied. It went on until the day her cell got switched off and kept switched off till today, implying probably Sonia changed her mobile number. The same happened with Orkut, where I went to her profile and was shocked to see in the left side it was showing "add as a friend" in her profile, meaning she had deleted me from her friends list. And when I wanted to scrap her a message popped "you can't create this scrap javascript (0)" whatever it means. I think she blocked me on yahoo messenger and gtalk also and also blocked my email id. So she wanted to throw me totally out of her life. At this moment I was feeling that orkut is just like our real lives. When we add friends on orkut we have to approve from both sides. And when we have to delete a friend any one can delete it and it will be deleted from both the sides. Only one person is required to break the friendship but adding requires consent(spelling) of two. And in our case the breaking element was

Sonia.

Well! It was true every time an SMS came to my cellphone, I dreamt of getting her SMS, but ended up getting an airtel offer SMS. I regularly checked her profile and downloaded every new pic she put in her album. I had this mania of collecting Sonia's snaps as the kids have for collecting stamps. And I also regularly read her scraps to know about her and to check whether there was any other guy in her life. And I re-re-read the chats, the chats that we did on yahoo messenger, when we were together. Yes, I saved all of those chats.

Can I get her back ever? Even after all this? Maybe I was thinking for the impossible. I was lost in these thoughts.

I couldn't sleep. I was just lying on the bed and changing sides. Sonia was floating in my eyes and dreams; her eyes, her voice, her patent dialogues, everything. Every moment spent with Sonia was recorded in my million GB brain. I just had to press the play button to see those video-graphic memories. Besides those I had 200 videos with her and about 500 pics of her stored in PC. Is having a good memory always good thing? I think, NO.

And it was her birthday on the next day, September Eleventh. And I was waiting for this day since her last birthday. I had saved Rs 1000 for her gift. I know the money wasn't that big but it wasn't too bad considering I saved it from my own pocket money. With it, I wanted to gift her something which would dissolve our misunderstandings and lead to patch-up. The gift should be like as soon as she unwraps it, she would jump and says "Oh Rahul loves me so much" and come back to me as happens in Bollywood movies.

But what it could be? I was thinking lying on my bed and listening to 107.8 fm. Viks, my room mate had already slept as the clock showed 3 am. RJ played one of my favourite tracks "Who Let The

Dogs Out". I was enjoying the song with closed eyes. Suddenly a bulb glowed inside my skull "DOG". Great ideas always comes either in bathroom(Archimedes) or when you're sleeping(Newton). Ya! She loved dogs like anything. The best word to describe her was she was dog-o-maniac. What could be a better gift than dog itself? It may sound as a weird idea at the first thought, but it was feasible. Gifting it at her house was safe, as she only lived with her mom and a puppy Max. I went there 3-4 times before our break-up and I think her mom liked me.

But where would I get a dog in Kolkata? Whenever I'm in any sort of such troubles, I follow only one mantra -"Go for Google". I typed "puppy Kolkata" in search bar of google.com and pressed enter. I had to browse between the links, but ultimately got address of a puppy house in Park Street. I joined community "Google Lovers" on Orkut just after that to pay google a homage. What a search engine!!!

The next thing which struck me is better known as ego and self-respect. Should I do this? Was I not letting myself fully under her? She was the one who left me. I knew a few mistakes were mine, but I said enough sorrys for what I did. But I knew she ~~is~~ was angry but ~~she is~~ not a betrayer. Strange random thoughts were swirling in my mind.

Should I tell Viks, Sid and Yash about it? But what would they think in this matter? Viks would laugh at me for doing all this even after being kicked like football. Sid would say something idiotically hurting. And Yash would give long speeches on self-respect, self dignity. But for me love was superior to selfdignity. If the love was true then can't we compromise a little on self respect? Well some of you might not agree with me, but I don't care. If put in my shoes even you'd be equally desperate to do anything.

I thought of hiding the whole thing from everyone. And if everything goes correctly and I get her back, I would tell them a whole cooked up story. I would tell them that Sonia came back to me realising her mistakes. But would the dog have such an impact that she'd come back to me, was the million dollar question.

I typed a senti-mail, printed it and shift+ deleted it. We had common computer and I didn't want to get caught. In the letter I typed all the sad senti dialogues of 'missing you', trust, love and all. Then I locked the letter in my suitcase. I wished I could give Black-cat security to the letter.

8

"I want a good dog" I said to the shopkeeper as I reached the puppy house in Park Street the next day.

"What's your budget sir?"

"Around 1000"

"I think Spitz would a good dog for you and it costs only Rs 1100"

I didn't know anything about dogs. Every dog was the same Tommy and Tiger for me.

"Show me the puppy. I want white furry one"

"This species comes mostly in white"

"What do you want male dog or bitch?"

"Male" I said. I had encountered with enough of the bitches in the past one month, Sonia's friends.

He showed 5-6 Spitzes. I chose the most innocent among them so that it could prove my innocence on my behalf.

"Please adjust a little bit in the cost. I'm a student and stay in hostel. I can't pay that much." The typical dialogue I used in every bargain. I can't bargain by any other method.

"Student? Hostel? What will you do with this puppy?" His asked as if I was a butcher and his concern was genuine.

"I'm gifting this to my aunty. She loves dogs" I defended myself.

"Okay you pay 1000"

Now puppy was with me, objective one was completed. Next objective was to deliver this puppy at her doorstep. Taxi? Too Costly. Bus? Very crowded. Auto? Doesn't go direct. So I was left with only one option, metro. Yes! Her house was at ten minute walking distance from Kalighat Metro.

I kept it in a gunny bag, so that no one sees it. And I kept the mouth of the bag open, so that puppy doesn't get suffocated. I got in the Park Street Metro and took the tickets for Kalighat.

We can hide a dog but not its basic instincts. He pissed from the carry bag while I was in the metro.

"Your bottle is leaking" A fellow passenger said.

I kept the bag on the floor. The very next moment the puppy started walking out of the bag. But he was half the bag's length and before he could come out, I lifted the bag again.

The puppy tumbled inside the bag and did exactly which I didn't want-"Bow Wow" He barked. My fellow passengers jumped aside startled.

"I heard dogs bark. Is it inside the metro?" An old man asked.

"It is with this guy. Inside the bag" Someone replied.

"Is it allowed inside a metro?"

"I don't think so. He should be fined"

They made it a huge issue and had a parliament meeting on it.

This is what old people love to do-scold and grumble at us for anything, they just need an excuse.

"Sometimes they have bombs inside pets and use them as pet-bombs. This is the latest kind of bombs, I saw in a news channel" Another old man said. I was feeling stifled. Thanks God! My destination Kalighat metro arrived a minute later and I got down quietly. I entered her house at 8:30 pm. I knew this was the time the guard or watchman of her apartment wouldn't be there.

Entering her house, I had three things, a basket in which I kept the blue-ribbon-tied puppy(blue being our common favourite colour); the senti-mail; and the MB or mistake book where I wrote all my faults, all the mistakes which I committed. I couldn't believe myself that it took seven pages to write all of my mistakes. I was sure that these three items together was a great recipe for a big banging into someone's heart.

I climbed the stairs to the fourth floor, where she lived. I saw the dog before keeping and said "my mascot, bring my love back" and kissed the dogs head.

As I was going to keep the puppy on the doorstep, all hell broke loose. Her dog Max began to bark. She already had a dog in her house which probably smelled his homo-species and started barking terribly. I got frightened. What to do next? I lifted the puppy and began to run downstairs.

Suddenly it struck in my mind, why was I taking the puppy back? I had to gift it to her. But with Max's barking becoming more and more fierce I couldn't get the courage to go upstairs to her floor. I kept it on 2nd floor and ran away. You know, I was a racing champion. I got a consolation prize in racing in class seventh. The stairs were really steep and I lost my balance and fell on my knees. It hurt but it wasn't the time of looking at my wounds. I was racing against myself as I was afraid of being caught with such an unwieldy thing. I looked behind to see if anyone was following me. Every second was passing like decades. I wished I had Mr. India's gadget so that I could become invisible. I stopped running after half a kilometre.

Operation dog was accomplished, though not very correctly. I kept it on the second floor, but it had a label around its neck on which Sonia's name was written. I was waiting for her call.

Ten minutes later my cellphone rang. Blinking on the screen was Sonia's landline number. Oh! She saw the gift and wanted to say me thank-you.

"What do you think of yourself? Huh? " It wasn't Sonia but her mom. What did she want to say?

"Take your dog back immediately" She said virtually shouting.

"Keep it for tonight aunty. I'll take it tomorrow" I said hesitatingly. I quickly planned in my mind that if Sonia kept the dog for one day, she would fall in love with the dog and then with me. I was becoming such a dog!

"Come and take back right now. I'm giving you fifteen minutes. If you don't come I'm calling the police." She said and kept the phone.

Police? Does police sit in her pocket or what? I was not too far from her house and returned back in ten minutes. Aunty was standing near the puppy on the second floor. And Sonia-I don't know where she was.

"What drama are you doing? Tell me what do you want to start?" Aunty said shouting.

"Why did you do this?" Aunty again.

"Aunty it was Sonia's birthday and I wanted to gift her something which she likes the most" I said.

"You don't have to worry about her so much. I know you're disturbing her now-a-days very much. You SMS her, call her"

"Disturb?"I was a little perturbed by the word disturb. When did I disturb her? If I wanted I could easily block her path anywhere and could create a scene. But I loved her and didn't want to make her feel odd. And where did the word disturb came from? When we were in relationship, I always called her many times each day, and I was doing the same, so was it 'disturbing'?

"Yes you disturb her so much, that she had to change her mobile no. I know everything. And now you are coming with this dog. And you kept this on the second floor. You wanted to create a scene? You know we live in an apartment? Thank God second floor people have gone somewhere or else it would have been such a humiliation. And you are so pitiless that you separated the small puppy from its mother? And you kept it here; what if the small puppy fell down the stairs?" Aunty was shouting non-stop; loudness increasing after each sentence.

I was startled by the unexpected consequences of my deed. And the way aunty was saying hurt all the more. She was more concerned about the dog than me. Every woman in this world knows how to hurt men.

"Aunty I'm sorry. I didn't intend to do anything like this. You know I and Sonia were such good friends."

"You were. But not now. One it is over, it's over. Don't drag it anymore."

And after that I said the dialogue which would win the best dialogue of the year if said in a bollywood movie. It would explode the theatre's ceiling out of people's claps and bring flood of tears in the theatre. The dialogue which would melt the hearts of all the women "Ami aapnar jonno bangla seekhchilam" (I was learning bangla for you people). Let's see what her response to this was.

"I don't know anything. You disturb her once more and I'll lodge police complaint against you. Mind you"

Police? Police? And what did I do? Did I commit any crime or what? I was just trying to get my lost love back. If love was a crime then I was a criminal. Seriously I was not afraid of police or anything but the thing which bothered was the bad impression I made on her. Was I so bad that she thought of calling the police?

"I thought you were a nice boy but what you did, really did prove me wrong. Get lost without delay and dare not do anything like this again" Aunty said her last few words and turned back.

The senti-mail which I kept with the puppy fell down. And I saw its last line which read "Relations doesn't get closer by meetings, but they are sweetened by thoughts. I care for you in my own strange ways. Maybe you'll never know. Maybe I'll never show. HAPPY BIRTHDAY"

I returned the dog to the puppy house. He was not ready to take it back. So I had to sell him back at half the price.

It was not the first time I was meeting aunty. I went to her house 3-4 times before this day. Aunty was very friendly and benevolent towards me. At this moment of time my videographic memory was playing the video of how it all started. How I met Sonia...

Photography Club

I kept my left foot first and then right as I landed. No it was not moon it was the classroom of photography club: one of the active students' club in Jadavpur University. Since the last one month, I always have been overcautious because I was in a new place Kolkata, that too a metro. By the way I'm Rahul; you must have heard the name.

I and Yash were least interested in photography; we actually joined the club for two reasons: -

(a) We were new in Kolkata and the club took us to places like Victoria, Alipore zoo etc for the practical classes, so we were able to visit some places in Kolkata (and that too for FREE!) FREE things always attracted my visual receptors since childhood. I still remember I used to buy the comics which had free stickers with them and those relishes of Bournvita(caps) which had toys free with them. And this time too I couldn't resist the power of FREE.

(b) Girls!!! Yes, Girls were aplenty in the club, especially Gurlz of arts faculty and that too of different flavours, colours and textures. We have this added advantage over other engineering colleges in the country.

There was strong rumour of arts girls joining the club in bulks.

Viks, the sports quota guy, who was my roomie also joined to accompany us.

Sid also joined with us, but his objectives were different. He wanted to learn photography as he would be requiring it in industrial training and in higher studies and to add one more point to his credentials in his CV. Typical bookworm he was.

We occupied the fifth bench in the first theory class of the club as it was at the centre and would facilitate us to watch pretty girls all around (Yash's geometrical funda). We reached early to the class by 10 minutes so that we don't miss anything (or rather anyone).

"Hey! It's only five minutes left and I can't see any pretty girl yet. Where are the goodies gone?" Yash said.

"Good things come at last" I said.

"Man you were right, check the duo" Yash noticed. He had excellent binocular eyes and great observation skills. Two girls were entering the classroom. One was wearing white and other pink.

"The pinky is cute. Whitie is good too" Yash said and I nodded. We had our special nomenclature system for girls. We called the girls by the colour of the clothes in which we saw them first.

I noticed the big eyes of Pinky which were looking like big cherries in small oval face. Whitie was fair and cute too. They both were the two best girls in the club.

When there was a talk about girls it was only me and Yash who had conversations. Sid didn't know anything except his studies and

Viks was not that interested in girls. Ya sometimes he eyed girls with us but when it came to love and relations he stood far away. According to him girlfriends were wastage of time and money. He was more interested in sports owing to his built up, six feet and three inches and weight beyond our calculation range. He looked like WWE champion(or human version of cross breed of girraffe and elephant) Here's how Viks proved girlfriend = evil.

Girlfriend = time x money

Time = money

Girlfriend = money2

Money = root cause of all evil = v(evil)

Girlfriend = (vevil)2 = evil

Don't get carried away, we were not fantastic four. Ya, we all were in same dept but we were just acquaintances. Viks was my roomie but his habits and attitude were totally different from mine and were very irritating. I wished I had a roomie like Yash, who was music crazy like me. But he was too rich to stay in hostel. He stayed in a two-bedroom flat in a big apartment. He had fundas and money and guitar. Wow!!!

Sid was a localite and lived at Salt lake with his parents. His Gandhiji like oval frame and Gandhigiri, both irritated me. His childlike attitude and over-sincerity also added to my exasperation. Sid was a kid. I talked to him for only two things, his notes and his Tiffin box.

"Camera is mainly divided into three parts" the instructor of the club started.

He taught the basics of photography, types of camera, F-stop no, exposure, focal length, aperture, zoom. The class got over in an hour.

"This Sunday we'll be going to Victoria Memorial. Gather at gate no. 2 at 7 am" The instructor said.

We came back to our hostel just after that. Attending photography classes after our regular lectures was really hectic. After one hour we got back to our real work which was preparing assignments, lab reports and last but not the least ED sheets. Graphics or ED (Engineering Drawing) or project and spatial drawing- are different names of the same devil. It was the most tedious, laboured and troublesome subject and the Prof made it more excruciating. He gave us atleast one ED sheet every week which may increase from upto five as per his discretion.

My drawing skills were extraordinary since my childhood. Whatever I drew looked no less than M F Hussain's modern art. But our Profs were traditional, so I had to put extra effort in ED. We struggled with our T squares, drafters and set-squares till 2 am.

I was sleeping cosy in my bed on Saturday morning when Nani called up

"How are you beta?"

"Pranaam Nani. I'm fine" I spoke with a yawn.

"Are you still sleeping? It's 8 am. You should be studying now." My nani was really strict and so was my nana with whom I used to live before coming here. They preserved the Brahmin culture even in this modern world. Waking up at 6 am was a compulsion because of my nana's military rule.

"I studied till late-night." I said defending myself.

"No big deal. It's expected of you. Study Hard!" She said

"I'll study" "I have to tell you something. You go and meet Mr.

Tiwari's family. They live in Dum Dum. They are very good people. They will care for you and will act be your local guardian from now on."

"Who are they?"

"They are my sister's daughter's husband's brother's...." She went on. {formatting}

"Ok Ok I got it" I interrupted in between. Don't know how can anyone comprehend that long chain of relation? The part of brain which processes relations is vestigial in my case.

"But it would be quite odd to go and meet somebody you don't even know" I said

"They are nice people. I have talked to them. Don't think so much. You'll have to pay them a visit on Sunday. No arguments"

"Sunday? But Sunday is tomorrow. How can I go? Do they know me?"

"Yes I've told them everything about you. And I'm SMSing their address to you?"

"Have you learnt typing SMS?" I asked. It was hard to imagine my nani typing SMS as she knew nothing except seizing my cellphone during exam time.

"Not me. Disha will do it. I'm keeping. Bye"

Disha was my six year old cousin. Modern kids learn technology faster than these oldies.

I slept again after hanging nani's call and got up again at 9:30 for getting ready for the 10:20 class. Everyone was busy in getting ready but Viks.

"Get up Viks. Its 10:10 now" I shook Viks terribly at 10:10. I was almost ready till then.

He opened his eyes, thought something. Then got up with a jerk and inserted brush in his mouth. In two minutes his brushing got completed and he splashed water on his face. Then he put jeans and shirt in 30 seconds and he was ready in 2.5 minutes. Better than Guinness book of world records. And natural calls, he attended mostly in the dept.

As far as bathing was concerned he was preservationist and strong supporter of saving water. Leave bathing, he probably hadn't changed his undies since past one week as one of his two undies was hanging outside. And he had only two.

If these things were left aside Viks was Okay. Though he didn't stink owing to overdosage of buy 1 get 1 free powder, but I stayed atleast a metre away from him.

On Saturday we had half days and we had to submit our ED sheet. KD sir came to the ED lab. The prof whose name petrified us.

"Show me your sheets. You first" He said pointing towards me. I was the first victim. I opened the sheet and waited for his response.

"What is this?" He said while making a 20 cm dia red circle on my sheet.

"And what is this?" Another red circle got made on my sheet

"This is ridiculous" another 5-6 circles.

My sheet was bleeding here and there due to KD Sir's knife like red pen.

"You can't get good marks with this quality of drawing." He stopped to think and then continued "I'll give you 5.9"

5.9? Was it the result of 10 hours of intensive labour? The only thing which satisfied me was I crossed pass marks of 5. This meant I was safe from repeat or RE, or in other words I would not have to do this drawing again.

But he was still pressing the sheet hard with his palms and thinking very deeply. Was he reconsidering his marks? Yes Sir, I deserved more.

He cut 5, wrote 4 followed by a decimal and a 9.

"4.9" He said.

"Tch tch tch. It's pitiable you failed by just point one marks" He finally said before handing me my murdered effort. And when he should have given me grace 0.1 marks, he failed me by 0.1 marks.

45 out of 80 in our class got RE, including Viks and Yash. Sid's got 8 which was expected from the topper.

ORKUT was one thing we got addicted to. We needed a minimum of two hours dose daily. Scrapping our friends and searching new 'single female Kolkata' became our favourite quest. And there was comparison of number of scraps. Sid was out of the competition with just 158 scraps.

"I have 2000" Viks said

"I have 2450" Yash replied.

"I have 2600" I said. "plus 10 testimonials and 38 fans" I added with an air of conceit.

"I have 40 fans. And don't worry. Wait for one week and I'll reach 3000" Yash said.

We had first of the four photography club practical classes on Sunday. We were to go to Victoria memorial. Pinky was just standing beside me. She was wearing white and her friend wore pink, as if they had exchanged their dresses.

Pinky was looking more beautiful than that day. I scanned her from all angles. Slim body, five feet three inches (manageable even by my standards), very fair, gorgeous, angel like face, what else could I have asked for. She was so fair that if she wore white it would be difficult pointing which shade was lighter her skin colour or white. Big eyes, thin eyebrows, small cute face, long hair and that killing smile. Oh I was going to die in a few moments. But the problem with me was that I had never approached any girl before. Ya, I had several school crushes but I never got the courage to go and talk to my dream girls.

Yash noticed me staring at her. He came behind me, put his hand on my shoulders and asked "Do you like her?"

"She is beautiful" I said as nothing else came to my mind. I didn't know anything about girls, how to talk to them or anything else.

"Want to talk to her?" he asked

"Ya" I said with my tongue rolled out like a dog.

"I'll teach you. Not now. How about next time" He said.

After returning from Victoria I had to visit Dum Dum to see the so-called-local guardian. I was clueless about bus routes so I chose taxi.

Sitting in taxi my brain was occupied with numerous questions? What will I say to Dum Dum family? How to talk to someone you've never met?

Dum Dum

"Tiwari Uncle?" I enquired.

"Rahul?" Uncle asked in reply.

"Come in beta" He said opening the door.

"Sit here" He pointed towards a Harappa culture sofa, or at least that old I guess.

"How is your life going on? How's been the last one month in Kolkata?" He started talking to me as if he knew me from my childhood. C'mon uncle, we're meeting for the first time.

"Fine" I said, still feeling very uncomfortable. I was observing his pitcher shaped tummy. He just wore a Janev in his top half of the body and rest he was wearing a green and white checked lungi .

"Rima! Get some sweets for Rahul" He shouted.

"Your nani called me and said you are doing engineering from JU" He continued

I nodded in affirmation. Whenever someone asked about JU, my chest puffed with pride.

"Donation or merit?" Was his next question and my smile sublimated.

This wasn't the question that people generally asked me. Leave praising, he was insulting me. And how can one expect donation when JU's fees is as low as rs. 2500 p.a.

"No uncle. I'm from merit. And I don't think they take admission through donation in JU." I defended.

"Never mind but now a days most of the engineering colleges take admission through donation, that's why I asked. Education is business these days. By the way, is your course a degree or diploma?" Another shocker and my eyes almost got wet. I wanted to leave the house then only. Was I here to get humiliated?

"Degree. A four year course" I somehow managed to say something, overcoming the shake up.

"Excellent beta. So we are sitting with a good future engineer" He said. "Rima! Where are the sweets?" He shouted.

"Coming" Aunty shouted in reply.

Aunty came with a tray full sweets of green colour. Wait, sweets of green colour! Was it p....? Oh it was *Parwal* – the vegetable I hate the most.

"Take beta" She said forwarding the tray towards me. She was wearing a brown sari and had big sindur lining on her head. Her nose and ears were pierced but she wasn't wearing any ornaments. She was only wearing a pearl necklace.

My hand nearly started shaking. I was really shy and nervous so I took one and somehow finished it.

"Take one more" This time uncle said.

"No uncle I don't like sweets much" I saved myself.

"Ok then let's have lunch. You must be hungry" He said.

Yes I was really hungry like a beast and mention of food watered my mouth. I was going to have home cooked food after one month. Hostel's food is, as you all know, seriously appalling.

Aunty brought the whole items starting with rice, dal and aalu dum, but the last item she brought really traumatized me. It was *parwal* ki sabji. My hunger disappeared. *Parwal* -I ate only once in my life and guess what, I took it all out, threw up. I simply can't swallow it.

I could have told them about my feelings but was feeling shy. Plus my nani being a very strict guardian instructed me not to waste a single bit of food, as food was God's gift to us and wasting was sin. This was a total bullshit for me but this is the price I had to pay because of my birth in a Brahmin family.

"Finish the worst item first" was my policy so that I can save better items for the end and change my taste. So I put the *parwal* into my mouth and swallowed it with water.

"Yippie! I finished it. Now I can eat somewhat peacefully" I said to myself. Though the aalu dum also didn't taste that good, but I continued happily.

One shouldn't too happy with anything because the devil forces attack you with disasters, I read somewhere; and the same happened with me.

"Beta. You like *parwal* very much. Don't you?" aunty said observing my *parwal* stock getting over.

"Don't feel shy. I have made a lot for you. Have more" Said aunty.

"No aunty. Please. I don't want more" I said frightened.

But why would aunty listen, she thought I was feeling shy. This time she gave me double the amount she gave the first time. Surveying the amount I started sweating.

"Now I'll have *parwal* at last" I said in my mind after my first policy failed.

After the lunch, I was watching the things around in their home. There were lots of books, few medals etc in the room. "Narmadeshwar Tiwari has been awarded an MA in English" I saw a laminated certificate hanging. I took out a few from the rack and read it to pass time.

"Come to this room Rahul" Uncle called me

It was the TV room. I was excited to watch TV after so many days. In our hostel, first years were not allowed to watch TV in the common room. Uncle was watching a news channel. A lady was narrating news and headlines were scrolling in the bottom two lines of screen. I was least interested in news except sports news.

Don't know at which line scrolling down uncle said "See the beauty of language. The transferred epithet is so beautiful"

I didn't know what transfer epithet was. I just kept quiet. I was afraid if I would ask uncle this he would think I've come from donation.

"See the alliteration" he said at another headline. I gave another blank look yet nodded like understood. And this was going on and on. Next he started discussing politics with me, which I hate the most. "You know the politics is getting worse day by day". There was a long discussion (one sided) on Laalu, Bihar, Sonia and all. Two hours passed and he was nowhere near stopping. My energy level fell and I was about to faint when a boy entered the room, probably Vishal, their son.

He went to aunty and whispered in her ears "Is he Rahul Bhaiya?" and aunty told yes.

"Hi bhaiya. Let's go to another room and talk" He said smilingly with his braced teeth.

I was looking upon Vishal as my saviour. We went to the other room away from those English language and political lectures.

"I handed him the packet of chocolate I bought for him"

"Why did you get this? It wasn't required" He said almost snatching it with his rod like hands. His hand was only bone and skin.

"Do you watch Noddy shows on cartoon TV?" Vishal asked eating the chocolates.

Now what was this? Cartoons? He was in class 10th and at his age I loved watching FTV and similar channels, I wondered how he can be so childish.

"What cartoons do you see then?"

"I don't watch cartoons"

"Have you played Max Payne II. And Duke Nukem?" He asked.

Computer games? What was he thinking of me. Maybe he was taking me as his friend. Probably I looked underage owing to my vertically challenged structure.

"Do you have girlfriend?" I asked changing the topic.

"No. I don't have girlfriend. Do you watch poppie the sailorman?"He was back to his normal set of questions; probably he also inherited some of his father's head eating genes.

Aunty called for dinner and food was as bad as expected and parwal made it worse.

In the night I and Vishal had to sleep in one room and he started again "Have you played Harry Potter game?"

"I'm feeling sleepy. We'll talk about this tomorrow." I said

"Have you played Alladin II?" He asked. He was such a shameless. Even when I told him I want to sleep, he didn't stop. I wrapped the pillow tightly over my ears.

When I got up in the morning, I was desperate to leave. Uncle and Vishal were still sleeping, only Aunty was awake.

"Have something and then go" Aunty said.

"No aunty. It's not required"

"Atleast sweets"

"No aunty. I haven't brushed my teeth. I can't eat" Thanks God! I had a point or else I would have to have *parwal* sweets again. I got out from the haunted house.

We had the second theory class of photography club on Friday.

"You want to talk to Pinky na?" Yash said.

"I'll make your way. You trust me?" He asked.

I nodded as I didn't have any option other than trusting him. Plus he seemed to be jack of these trades.

Three minutes were left in beginning of class. But where the hell were Pinky and Whitie?

"Last day she sat on the second bench of the left row." Yash started calculating on paper. He made a rough map of classroom, showing rows and columns of benches.

"Three minutes are left and middle row is full up to first six benches, right row up to eight and left up to only two. Girls like to sit in the front. So she will sit on the third bench of the left row"

"Go and sit on the third bench of left row"

"What to do after that? I mean how to start conversation with her?"

"You sit there without your notebook and ask her for pages. This will start your conversation."

"And in case my calculation goes wrong and she sits somewhere else, we are keeping a seat for you with us. Just taking safe side, my calculations never go wrong."

"Go and sit on the third bench of left row. And keep this N-series with you. It'll give a good impression." Yash said after a pause.

I did exactly what Yash said. She entered the class and I couldn't believe it, It happened! Yash's calculation went cent percent accurate. She sat beside me and whitie sat near her. No! There was no rainfall of flowers. It's real life, Okay?

The class started. Everyone started writing except me. I started looking at her copy with needy greedy eyes, as per the plan.

"Can you give a piece of paper?" I asked acting or over-acting shy. I tried some bollywood learnt techniques of looking shy. She smiled and tore a middle page from her copy and handed over to me.

I wrote in the biggest fonts without getting noticed and finished off the page and then I saw on her copy like a hundred day hungry puppy. She gave me page again.

Class got over and she left. I couldn't do much. Neither did I ask her name nor anything. But whatever I did was like an achievement if compared to my school life.

Coming out from the class I thrashed the paper in the dustbin. Its purpose was over now. Happy with the success of created coincidence of Yash, which made me talk to Pinky today.

Yash was really a great guitarist which I came to know when I went to his flat one day. I really liked visiting his flat because it had everything one would like to have, Laptop, TV, iPod and ya, Fridge, I liked drinking chilled water.

He was busy playing the chords of summer of '69 of Bryan Adams and humming along with it. I joined him with my voice. He had that beautiful sleek red electric guitar like Yash's sleek body. He also stuck many tattoos on it which made it look enigmatic. And the projected part of the strings were cut and curled like curly long hair of Yash. And Yash was giving special sound effects and distortions, which only electrical guitar can give.

"Let's make a band. We'll win all medals" I said jokingly when the song ended.

"Band. Yes I was also thinking of it. It's time to give it a serious thought." Yash said.

Serious thought? But I was joking, seriously, I was joking. I'm not a trained singer, but Ya, I can perform well in bathroom. But outside it, I had no experience.

"You know, I had my school band. But here I don't know anybody." Yash said tuning up his fourth string.

"India lacks good rock bands. Parikrama is one. This is the reason of instant success of Jal Band. We need more bands like that" I said changing the topic. Generally speaking of problem is easier than finding the solution.

"Ya. Rightly said. We have these good local bands here and in north east like Fossils and Cactus. But most of them perform either in local language or English songs. We need bands to perform Hindi rock numbers." Yash said.

"But I'm going to form my band, this is for sure." Yash said very firmly and with deep earnest feelings. And I also mused with amusement.

AC Canteen

Sunday morning brought the second practical class of photography club. Though 6 am was too early, I was enthusiastic enough to get up at right time. I woke up Viks too, though it took several attempts. We reached at gate no 2, from where the club would reserve a bus for the suburbs of Kolkata. Natural scenery would provide us a lot of photographic opportunities there, some senior told. It was 7:10 and students were still coming as 7:30 was the deadline to join for the trip.

{please check the formatting of next few lines} "Hey Rahul! Here comes your Pinky?" Yash said with his eagle eyes.

"Oh. Ya" I said with my eyes wide open.

"Try your luck today. Go and talk."

"But what will I talk about? Don't have any excuse like paper and pen today." But just before when we were to take the bus, it started raining cats and dogs. It was strange how it rained as the sky was clear in the morning. Meanwhile Sid's SMS came on Yash's cell "I can't cum 2day bcz of rain and studies.". I was least bothered as Sid's presence hardly mattered. "Never trust weather and girls. They are most unpredictable in this world." Viks said.

With rain on its full strength and we without our shields to fight rain, it was natural for us to get wet. I was happy because the rain made Viks bath forcibly after 20 big days, maybe he was sad.

I noticed Pinky opening her umbrella. Being a local maybe she was prepared for erratic rains. Yash noticed me gazing her.

"Why are you getting wet when she has umbrella?" He said patting my back. I understood what Yash said and walked towards her.

"Hey you! Hi. How are you? I forgot to say thank you that day" I said. Yash taught me a great funda, always keep the last conversation incomplete so that you can start from the same place. Always keep something for the next talk.

"You're always welcome. How are you?" She replied.

"You can see" I pointed to my wet clothes

She smiled and said "You can come under mine."

Yes! This was what I wanted. Standing with a beautiful girl under umbrella was really romantic, like I saw in Bollywood movies. I like movies and so I like things filmy.

A senior announced the news of cancellation of the trip because of rain. Instead the class was to be held now in JU itself, as JU also has lots of trees and greenery.

"Let's go inside the campus" I said finally standing at five centimetre separation from the princess of my dreams. ED gave us a good idea of guessing distances roughly. Her scent was making me crazy. This was for the first time I was standing so close to a girl. I noticed that her cheeks were very shiny and soft. She had a slim, perfectly sculptured body(guessing from the external view only). She was looking completely like the Barbie-dolls. I wish I could pack her and keep with me forever.

As we were walking together I said "What is your name by the way? I forgot to ask that day."

"Sonia Bose" she replied.

"And what's your department? You're from arts, I guess."

"Ya. I'm sociology student. And you?"

"Rahul Sharma. Automobile engineering department"

She started questioning "You're not from Kolkata. Are you?"

I feel uncomfortable when someone takes the stand of asking questions and I've to answer.

"No I'm from Ranchi."

"So how're you feeling here?"

"Okay till now. But how do you study socio? I think socio is a head-ache subject." I said snatching the hold of questioning. And I knew her reaction to this question won't be uninteresting.

"No socio is a nice subject and I like it." She said raising her eyebrows, as expected. She gave me get-out-of-my-umbrella look. Raising her eyebrows made her dark brown eyes wide and inexplicably beautiful.

"I don't believe you. I consider it as a subject of no use. There are huge lectures on a point of no meaning. Sometimes they even forget the topic on which they are giving lecture. It's like things are all muddled up."

"No it's not like that. Actually it is......It is...I can't explain, but it's good and I like the subject" She said shielding herself.

Meanwhile someone shouted my name and I turned. Yash was waving his hand to call me.

"Excuse me. You keep going. I'm coming in two minutes." I said to Pinky, now Sonia.

"Okay" she said.

As I reached Viks said "Ask for her email id etc or better ask whether she is on Orkut?"

"You all are still kids. Go to phone number straightaway. This is 21st century man" Yash said.

"Phone number?" I and Viks raised our eyebrows in unison.

"Yes. What's the big deal?" Yash said.

"How will I ask her phone number? What if she refuses to give?" I enquired.

"Ideas man! Ideas! If you've got correct ideas you would never fail." Yash said making gestures like magicians.

"What ideas are you talking about?" I asked.

"Never ask for a phone number, always give yours" He said this with the same expression which physics sir gave after proving the theorems.

"How does it make a difference? Will it work?" I asked.

"Girls are to be dealt with reverse psychology. Look, when you ask a girl her number, her defences go up and she puts guards on herself. Now she is having a negative psychology towards you and so all your efforts fail. Now if you do the reverse, you don't ask her number, but give yours, she gets confused. This gets you free to attack your target. If still you can't understand what I'm saying then don't think, just do what I'm saying" Yash instructed.

I came back to Sonia. Today, we were divided in a group of six and the instructor again taught speed of film, exposure etc. I was in Sonia's group and used my whole energy to learn fast the things and act intelligent to impress her. This thing followed from school when I tried to get highest in Science and Maths to impress girls. Don't know they ever got impressed or not?

The class got finished in an hour. The rain stopped but it was still water logged in Jadavpur. Poor drainage system, you know. I was walking with Sonia again, swimming rather. We came out of gate no 3 and crossed the road while crossing the knee deep water.

While she was waiting for the auto I said

"I am new here. I don't have friends. Would you mind being in touch with me? I want to be in touch with you. Please take my cell no"

"Tell" She said

"9903102457" I told.

"Wait, I'm giving you a missed call" She said.

Yippie! Yash's tricks worked! She also gave her phone no by default. Yash had great understanding of women. He was a handbook of these cool ideas.

"I did it. Yo!" I shouted when I met Viks and Yash who were in a different group.

"Know *yaar*, I was feeling great walking with her under the same umbrella. It was so romantic" I said while we were returning to the hostel.

"No romantic *vomantic*. Actually you both looked like the old condom advertisement on DD-1" Viks teased and started singing "pyar hua ikaraar hua hai…"

"You bastard. I'll kill you" I said as I took my slippers off and ran after him hastily splashing water. Yash laughed unstoppably.

Monday first period was Physics. Professor entered the class with 4 chalks, all of different colours. He wrote on the board "BERNAULLI'S THEOREM"

He started with making a diagram with pink chalk. Then he labelled the diagram and assumed variables with yellow chalk. He then started proving the theorem with white chalk. Professors maintained to be colourful even in their late 50s.

"Let us assume a non turbulent flow of incompressible and non viscous liquid" Prof said.Assume is the favourite word of physics people. Everything is assumed and at the last it's told that the formula derived from assumed situation fits well in non-assumed situations also. I don't how does it happen?

He wrote in eight steps the entire proof. He got confused several times in the process and scratched his hairless head. And the moment he reached the end-"Hence Proved" he wrote this with the fourth colour chalk-blue. Probably he saved the best colour for the climax.

He was enormously happy. His face became red with delight as if he had just discovered this theorem in class. I was wondering if he would start shouting eureka eureka as Archimedes did. I wished I could clap for him and applaud on his success of re-inventing the wheel.

We had enough of these professors now. Next was English period and we took French leave. Thanks God for blessing us with Sid, who never missed any class and copied all notes sincerely and rendered us free to bunk some of the not-so-important ones.

In the free time we got we sat in the AC canteen. No, it was not air-conditioned; it was Amenity Centre Canteen -our common hangout place where we used to check out girls. Because of the essence of beauties its Rs. 3 coffee tasted better than Rs. 75 coffee of CCD.

"Hey look at browny." I said while we were sitting on the centre table. (Yash's geometry)

"She is gorgeous. Really beautiful" Yash said.

"Go and talk" I said.

"But what will I say?" Yash said.

"You just go. Ideas will come to your mind."I said. He was Yash after all. He with his cool ideas could get any girl he wanted.

"Go Go. She is alone" I pushed him while he was still in his thoughts.

He went to Browny. We hid behind the entrance and peeped how our fundu-man does it. Maybe it'll provide us some training.

Yash walked and asked "Excuse me! What's your department?"

What did he ask? He was looking awfully nervous. I thought it was wrong way to start. But maybe Yash had some idea.

"Why should I tell you?" The girl said in instant reply with a boldness that only beautiful girls possess.

"Good question!" Yash replied tautly. "Why should you tell me?" He shook his head. "Ok! Tata" He said this and came back to us with face dropped. I was expecting more from him. Maybe he would re-return and do something out of the box. But no, he was walking towards the door.Did this really happen?

He fumbled in front of this girl badly. One thing was clear Mr. Fundu was not so cool at executing his own ideas. But how did he bungle? I thought he was the coolest one.

"You *phattu*!" Viks teased. Yash was himself looking very disappointed.

"Hey I tried atleast" Yash defended himself.

"But you were the expert" Viks taunted again.

"And it's not that easy as it looks. Why don't you try it yourself? I don't think you can even talk as much as I did" Yash fortified again.

"I bet I can ask her name" Viks beamed.

"Forget it" Yash said.

"Bet?" Viks said with his palms open towards Yash, serious this time.

"100 rupees if you succeed in asking her name and come back without having her sandals. Girls are not your cup of tea. Handling girls require special skills." Yash said

"Skills that you displayed?" Viks said scoffingly stood up and went straight towards Browny. She was not alone this time. She was sitting with three friends around a table in other corner of the canteen. "You're beautiful" Viks said to the brownie straightaway.

"He's dead" Yash said with a smile mixed with worry.

"What?" The girl asked. Actually the girl was confused how to react. On one hand she was praised and on the other hand she had to be strict with boys.

"Never mind, I was just praising your beauty. You are the most beautiful girl in canteen" Viks said confidently.

She was trying to curb, but her smile was overflowing. All the surrounding friends were burnt to ash. Girl's jealousy you know.

"Can I know your name please?" Viks paused and said "By the way I'm Vikram, 1st year, dept of automobile."

"Ishika" She said with a smile on her face. Viks came back.

"Gutso. Hail Viks" Yash said to Viks.

"Gutso" I copied Yash.

"My 100 rupees?" Viks demanded.

How did it happen that Viks succeed and Yash botched? Yash was far better good looking than Viks. Though Viks was taller, but Yash was not short either (5'10"). Viks was dark but Yash was fair. And Yash had long hair and a stylish goatee. If points were given on looks, Yash woud have scored double than Viks. And Yash had his fundas which no one had. The only thing he lacked was confidence. At this point I assumed his confidence level was even lower than mine. And here was Viks not breathtakingly handsome but bold and strong. Confidence matters, I guess.

My Day Out

FOOTBALL ARENA MATCH is the World Cup of JU. All the departments participate in this annual football tournament with bursting emotions and ultra commitment. From the first year Viks got selected in the dept team, which was obvious and Yash also made through as extra player. It was doubtless that I was worthless.

The team practiced hard till the D-day arrived. We all surrounded the field before the start of match. Both Viks and Yash were in the team in the starting.

"Best Of luck" I said hugging Yash.

"Best of luck to you too" I waved thumbs-up for Viks. Sorry, I can't hug with his odour.

Both the teams were in their jerseys which must be making them feel proud, the pride I can never get.

The referee's whistled and the match started. The field was circumferenced by students, supporters and opponents' supporters. I don't like football match and I was getting bored, so I went to CET canteen to have something. Then I went to computer centre to do orkutting with proxy server.

"Goal!" The department roared. With more than 200 people hollering together, the ambience of the field was amazing and I could hear the sound inside the CC.

Roughly after ninety minutes of listening to the reverberation I came to the ground. The whole department lifted Viks except me. He made a hat-trick of goals. He was a true champion-Strong, confident, robust, stout but smelly. One thing was clear, whether it was girl or game, confidence matters.

I went on Yash's flat in the evening for listening to his new iPod. Apple iPods really have unbeatable sound quality.

"Rahul! Come here fast. What's the date today?" Yash shouted animatedly.

"10th sep. Why? What happened?"

"Your darling's birthday is 11th sep. See her profile."

"Who, Sonia? Okay I'll wish her tomorrow"

"Wish her today idiot. How many times have you called her till now?" Yash asked.

"Maybe 3-4 times. We mainly exchange SMS"

"This is the best chance you'd ever get. Girls love to be wished on their birthdays. And the one who wishes them first, wins the jackpot"

"Call her just now" Yiks said after a pause.

"It's 11:50 in the night. How can I call her so late? She is a girl. And she doesn't live in the hostel like us; she lives her with parents"

"No problem buddy. She must be wide awake; after all it's her birthday after 10 minutes. This is just the right time to call her and make her phone line busy. Her friends will also be trying her number after a few minutes."

I did what Yash said, called her, passed 10 minutes talking craps like how was your day and all. Yash blew whistle gently as signal and at sharp 12 and I wished her "happy birthday to you" I said this in more as a singing fashion.

"How did you know about my birthday?"

"That's not important at all. Tell me who else has wished you till now?"

"You are the first one" and I said yes almost in an instantaneous reaction.

"So it was your plan? Huh!"

"Yes I wanted to be the first one to wish you. And if I had called after twelve, your cell could have been busy. So I decided to call 10 minutes early"

"So where do u want the treat?" She asked.

"Treat?" I never expected that. I mean in our case we had to filch treats from friends, but she was willing to give treat herself. Wow!!!

"It's your birthday, you decide, plus I don't know anything here too, so I don't know" Viks and Yash were lazy bobs. They didn't want to do anything but sleep all the day. And Sid just traveled from college to home and Vice versa in S-9 and even studied in bus.

"Have you ever been to Inox forum?"

"Nah. Never"

"Come then. My friends will also come. Are you free tomorrow?"

Free? I was always free. And when beautiful girls were concerned I had all the time in this world for them. But I had to keep the reputation of my engineering degree, how could I be free?

"Let me check. 12th I have to submit report, 12th is viva ... Ya. I think I can manage it tomorrow. But with your friends, I won't feel comfortable." I mumbled.

"Then come 1-2 hours early. Come at 12:30"

"Okay, tell me how to reach there"

"Oh! I forgot. You're not familiar with Kolkata. Tell me where you can reach without getting lost"

"Am I a kid? Why will I get lost?"I said confidently but deep inside I knew my shallow reality.

"Can you reach kalighat metro?"

"Ya. Why not? But how to reach there?"

"Oh! you don't even know kalighat? Take any of the bus among SD4, 1, 1A. It would take around half an hour. Will you be able to come there or should I.."

"I'll come" I intercepted.

"Okay then. 12:30, Kalighat Metro. Give me a missed call when you reach there" We Indians use missed calls to its fullest extent.

I wore my favourite blue coloured full shirt and black jeans the next morning. Though it was too hot in Kolkata but I wore full shirt because of my obsession for blue. Viks was enjoying his Sunday sleep I took this situation to full advantage and sprayed Viks's newly bought axe deo with the aim of emptying it.

Viks got the smell of his perfume and suddenly opened his eyes asking "Will you give her a gift? Don't spend much though. Give her some low-priced card or something."

"C'mon yaar, she is giving me treat me in a mall. I can't give her a gift like that"

"Mall" he thought for a second and continued "In any case always stay on the profit side. Spend less than she would spend on you". This cheapo can't tolerate anyone spending a penny on girls.

I went to shop and bought a Cadbury Gift Pack (universally acceptable gift) and got into SD4 bus. In the bus I told the conductor to stop at Kalight and then I told to driver also.I wasn't satisfied with this and I told all my fellow passengers to tell me when kalighat reaches. And that wasn't it, I kept asking them after every 5 minutes "Is this Kalighat". The whole bus knew where I had to get down. Maybe they were annoyed with me but I was too excited to notice them. I saw them in TV before but it was the first time I was to see a mall and metro train and that too with a beautiful girl! Ya I was electrified. The whole bus shouted in chorus when Kalighat arrived.

I called on her cell after getting down "Where are you?"

"I am on my way. Hey! I can see you. Bye." I saw all around but couldn't see her. I belong to a small place and always get afraid of the BIG things of Kolkata, its buildings, streets and all. I handed the Cadbury gift pack to her.

We entered the kalighat metro and she bought the tickets. She handed over my ticket to me and she went to the ticket-checking machine. She entered her magnetic ticket and crossed through the gate and went the other side. My legs were shaking out of nervousness. I entered the ticket but oh, the machine refused to take my ticket and beeped.

"Put it this way" She said.

I followed her instructions and the machine ate the ticket but ah, what to do after that? I pushed the gate hard but it refused to move. Maybe the machine was ragging me seeing that I was a first timer. She also couldn't help as she was on the other side. Lastly we had to ask a gentleman for help who let me enter with him with his ticket.

My confidence was shattered. Bad start, really bad start. What would be she think of me: an illiterate villager. I had to do something to shed my villager's image.

"Have you ever been to Delhi?" I asked Sonia as the metro train's door got shut and it left the platform.

"No I've never been. Why?"

"Delhi metros are far better than Kolkata metros. The metro is fully AC unlike here and there the entrance system is also quite different"

She smiled in reply and I couldn't figure out why.

Travelling in metro was a cake walk as compared to the entry. The metro was crowded. The thing I don't like Kolkata is its population. You can see rush and long queues everywhere.

"Beautiful" I said as we were getting down at Ravindra Sadan, breaking the noisy silence which was in metro. Actually I wanted to say that she was looking beautiful, but could just manage to say beautiful.

"What?"She narrowed her eyes and eyebrows. Probably she didn't hear what I just said.

"I said your dress is beautiful" I didn't have the guts to say what I wanted to.

She smirked amusingly.

"Ya it's really nice" I repeated my words.

We walked ~~to~~ out of the metro station. Kolkata is a strange place just 100 metres away from a multi-storeyed mall you can see dumps of garbage, slum and naked children. Kolkata has been perhaps developed in bits and pieces.

One kid was pulling the tail of a street puppy on the street. The puppy was crying and howling. Sonia ran to the kid and twisted the ears of the kid with her full force. The kid left the puppy's tail and started crying as the puppy did previously.

"How it feels when someone pulls your ears?" Sonia asked the kid.

"Leave her *na*. He is a kid"

"No. He is a to-be-monster. You see he is teasing this small dog so much. These demons need to be taught a lesson"

She was so concerned about the dogs. Which species does she belong to? And she was punishing a human for a dog. The kid started crying with tears now and his ears became blood red.

"Never do it again. Or else I'll come again" Sonia scolded the kid. The kid ran away even before Sonia could finish her sentence. We also got moving.

Ah! And here was Inox Forum -the breathtakingly beautiful mall. Beautiful not because of decorated shops but girls. I wished to stand and look around for a while but she was in a hurry, perhaps her friends were to come after sometime.

I somehow managed to walk on the ultra-smooth and slippery marble, but a monster awaiting me

was standing tall in front of me -the Escalator. You don't have to fumble. You have to do it correct this time. I told myself. And Voila! I stepped on it and to show my confidence I started stepping up on the already moving escalator. Another thing to prove my stupidity.

"You don't need to walk on a moving escalator." She said.

"It is moving very slow here. In Dehi escalors move very fast" Delhi again came to save me. But frankly speaking I had never been to Delhi either.

"What do you want to eat?" She asked as we entered the food corner of Inox, The BURP.

I never saw any of the items before and they had strange names too.

"It's your birthday. You should decide"

"No. It's my treat and you are here for the treat so you decide"

"Hakka Noodles" I said as I didn't want to try something new and make a fool out of myself.

"What with Hakka?" She asked

"Take anything"

"Baby corn?"

"Order it" What was this by the way?

We took a double seat or couple seat. We were sharing the baby corn in the same plate. It was somehow sort of romantic for me.

"What does your boyfriend do?" I asked. Yash told me this idea of indirect asking.

"I don't have boyfriend. What about you?" Hey! She was one of the endangered species(almost extinct) of kolkata-single beautiful girl.

"I also don't have a boyfriend either"

She laughed and said"What about girlfriend?"

What should I say now? 18 and still no girlfriend, may be that would sound shameful

"I had"

"And now?"

"I've lost touch after I changed school" A foreigner girl passed near our table. She was so fair, so beautiful. I had to concentrate on the food to keep me away from these distractions. I didn't want to get caught by Sonia eying other girls. I wished I was with Yash and Viks and this heaven would have got some good admirers

"Have you ever been on a date?"

"Yes many times. Many many times." Suddenly it flashed in my mind was this a date? What is a date? A girl and boy sitting in a couple seat in a mall, isn't it a date? Whatever it was, was first of its kind for me, maybe she has done this several times.

After we finished the food, she came with me to see me off till metro and help this moron cross the metro gate.

"Your dress is really looking beautiful. And you are looking beautiful too" Yes I said it finally! The door of metro got shut. She grinned and waved me bye.

I came back and reported the whole thing to Yash and Viks. I calculated the total amount she spent on me today. Viks was happy with the fact that I was in a 150 percent profit.

Experiments with Emotions

Though Yash was very poor in execution, but his ideas were still fresh and nifty. This time he gave an excellent idea to keep in regular touch with Sonia. This was necessary, as the photography club classes were over and I needed some way to stay connected with Sonia.

The plan was simple and Yash had named it – Experiment With Emotions. The need for this plan was felt on the day we got a report on Workshop Technology in which we had to make a lot of drawings in it. I was always awful at drawing since my childhood. Natural un-artist I was. Drawing was the only subject in which I performed very consistently (failed).How could I've done the figures of intricate shapes of Ball and peen hammer, C cramp, Bench vice etc. And the drawings carried 100 marks.

This is how it started when Yash said "If you want to get close to a girl, you have to take the path of emotions. You have to tame the fire of emotions running inside the girl's heart" he was ready with preaching like love guru. The fire and all about which he was speaking was beyond my understanding but I trusted him fully and followed his words like perfect disciple.

"You're listening to this guy? The guy who fumbled in front of Ishita. *Phattu!!*" Viks said

"You stay out of it. I trust Yash." I defended him "and how can you forget his photography club predictions?" This shut up Viks.

"Do at your own risk" Viks said.

"What were you saying? Continue" I asked

"Just wait and watch" Yash said.

"Hey I don't want to play with and hurt anyone's emotion. Sonia is a nice girl"

"It's nothing like hurting. You're just using the key of girls-emotions."

"You sure it won't hurt her? Exploiting another person's feelings is not good."

"Cent percent sure. After all the entire plan is well knitted by me"

After working for an hour he gave me the ingredients of the plan. He wrote down the plans, a step by step program in the form of a flowchart and gave it to me to execute it. Not in computer but real life.

I called up Sonia on her cell at 10 pm, as per the plan and asked her "I have my test tomorrow. I've to study tonight. Will you study tonight?"

"I too have a test tomorrow"

"Great let's play missed calls to keep each other awake. When you or I give a missed call, the other person has to give a missed call in return in sixty seconds. We can also SMS and call in between and talk to keep awake."

And we played missed calls and started SMSing each other every half an hour and called after one hour. In the 5-10 minutes call we talked about our likes and dislikes. This happened for 3 rounds.

Meanwhile Yash collected four of the saddest messages from his cellphone. He told me to forward these SMSes to Sonia.

"evrythng in this world is so divine, bt evrythn is nt mine.d only thng I thought my own was my tears, but they are also not mine" I SMSed

"hey!wht's wrng wit u?y r u sendin such dprssn msg?is evrythn alrite?" Pat came her reply. She uttered too many interrogatory sentences at one go.

"The message was very depressing which I chose deliberately. She also forwarded a message in reply. Then I again messaged a more depressing SMS and as expected she replied again. And her reply came within a minute. Girls type SMS so fast. *"Wht hpnd sdnly? Y u not tellin?"*

I knew exactly what to do now. I SMSed again a further more depressing SMS and as she called just after that

"Hey what happened to you suddenly?" She said as I picked the call.

"Actually my head is aching and I'm not feeling good"

"What happened suddenly? You were normal one hour before"

"Aah..Nothing" I spoke in a tone which would make anybody think that I was very much depressed (I am excellent at acting and making voices).

"Say something"

"What can I say Sonia? God plays great pranks with us. There are many problems which I don't discuss with anyone"

"But you can tell me" She said concerned.

"No I don't like sharing my problems. These are my share of problems"

"But problem decreases when you share them. "Please tell me your problem. Maybe I can help you"

"There is nothing to tell you. Talk about something else"

"No first you have to tell your problem" She said. Don't know why girls want to know everything, whether they are of any use or not.

"I can't tell you. It's better you leave me at my state and fate. Everyone has problems. I have some problems locked in a leak-proof tank but whenever someone hits over it it starts leaking or overflowing and it gives a lot of pain. Anyways leave my topic. You are fine?" I was just reading what Yash wrote for me.

"Yes I am fine. It's okay if you can't share your problem with me, but you should share your problem with someone. Right now you should go to sleep. When you'll sleep you will forget your problem for a while and get relaxed. I'm saying this with my personal experience"

"Okay mam. As you like it. It's late now. It's better you too go to sleep. Good night. Take care of yourself"

"You also take care. good night. Bye bye. And ya. Try to sleep. Take some sedatives if you have" she said and hanged phone.

As you all know, I had no tension or pain. I was extremely cool and composed. After talking to her I read some novels while listening to red 98.3 fm. After two hours I felt sleepy and went to sleep after putting my cell phone on silent mode.

"1 new message received" I saw on my mobile's screen just after I woke up. "*Hw r u feeln nw? Did u sleep? Did d slp help?*" I smiled as I got another opportunity to exploit and I replied "*Wht cn I do whn d sleep hs left me too? I couldn't sleep 4 a min n nw I hv a lil bit of fever too.*" Fever is the word to which the girls are too reactive and she immediately called again as expected.

"Why don't you tell me what happened to you"

"I told you, I can't tell"

"Fine! Don't tell then. But just look at you. You have become sick now, you have fever. Can't you see the problem is eating you from inside?"

"What can I do in this?"

"Take some medicines. Keep yourself well. Change your mood. Are you coming to college today?"

"Maybe"

"Then meet me. I'll tell you methods to divert your mind. I had psychology in 12th"

I got a chance to meet her! Can you believe it?

I met her during the lunch break.

"How are you feeling now?" She asked.

"It's better now. Fever has come down"

"I know you won't tell me your problems but I'll do my duties" She told me about some techniques of relaxation.

Seeking the correct timing I said "Can you do me a favour?"

"What?"

"I know you are good at sketching. Can you please do my drawings? I got a project. I am awful at drawing"

"Okay no problems." How could she deny, after all she had to cheer me up and lessen my problems.

"I know I'm troubling you with this. I'm really sorry for this. You can refuse if you wish"

"I'll slap you if you'll again talk like this" She said. I can't tell how good it felt from inside. The mention of slap meant the barrier of formality was over between us. Another milestone achived.

My multi-purposed plan was successful. I had to go to my home town for the next three days for a cousin's marriage. I told Sonia that I was going to change my mood. Sonia was frightened to see when I gave her the drawings to make. It was forty-six drawings, but she promised to do it in three days.

Two days later, from my home PC I was chatting with Sonia through yahoo messenger I said "Show on webcam. I want to see the progress of my drawings. And I also want to see that you are doing it correctly or not?"

She didn't want to do this. But when I insisted too much she had to search her webcam and then install it. And then turn her study lamp on as webcam didn't show clear pictures.

"Beautiful" I said when I saw the drawings and the artist behind it, referring to both of them.

"You know. You're the most annoying person I've ever known" She said.

"It has been suggested before" I replied

When I came back, I met her to take the sheets. She was standing at the entrance of Central Library.

She was looking stunning in black top. I took the whole sheets and just glanced at the whole stuff. The girl really worked hard. She drew those and pictures and shaded them also. I was sure I'd get an A for this. Whatever she did definitely deserved a treat.

Oh NO! But there was a blunder. She wrote "ANGEL" where we had to write ANGLE. And Profs would burn us alive if they found us writing angels in place of angles. And the treat got cancelled before even being declared.

But atleast I found a girl who would make my projects and all.

I went to Dum Dum again this weekend. There was nothing which pulled me there, but Nani who pushed me there.

I was feeling thirsty, so I opened the freeze to get some chilled water. I had visited here many a times now and I was familiar with everything.

When I opened refrigerator to drink water, I froze when I saw five packets of that sweets and rest of the fridge filled with raw *parwal.* Their love for this vegetable was remarkable. I doubted eating this much of *parwal* must have changed their anatomy and DNA structure. I wondered if their muscles were green. If endoscopy was ever done to their stomach the doctors would find green linings on the oesophagus and intestines.

By the way I must tell you, I was also eating *parwal* for past five months. It sucks if you are a person like me, too shy to say no to anyone. Aunty still thought parwal was my favourite too as was theirs.

As usual Aunty started cooking *parwal* in the evening. It was heights now and it was beyond tolerance limit. I had to do something to stop it. I quickly framed a plan in my mind.

I was in the TV room. Uncle smiled when he saw me, probably happy because he got his dinner, his jackpot, if you get what I mean.

Every time he I came here he used to deliver long speech to me, which I think was his deepest unfulfilled desire. Last time uncle gave lecture on engineer and society. Actually he was telling that now-a-days engineer does nothing for the society. They just work for the MNCs and IT and ITes which work for the US. They have very low moral values and blah blah blah. Once he started stopping him was almost impossible. I don't know why he hated engineers so much, especially engineers with MBA.

He went to other room to change clothes and started without brakes when he returned "See what government is doing these days. I always doubt their policies. Actually I want that...Rahul...Rahul"

And I was tightly closing my eyes, prefect acting of sleeping.

"Rina. Give him a blanket. He has slept. Has he eaten something?" Uncle said.

I smiled not on my face, but only in my mind. My trick was flawless.

"Rahul bhaiya has slept? Shit! I had to tell him so much" Vishal said. Ya he had to tell about those cartoons and games.

I was celebrating within the success of today. What a great victory it was – no parwal, no mindeating talks. Even though I had to sleep empty stomached, yet it was better than eating parwal.

I got up at 6:30 in the morning, unusual but safe time coz the whole family generally kept sleeping this early. I splashed my face with water. I was getting ready in a hurry but with soft paws so that I don't wake them. When I entered the drawing room to get my shoes on, I got drenched into sweat with fear. They were already awake and were sitting like hungry tigers to tell their stories in the morning.

"You slept very early yesterday. Were you tired?" Uncle asked.

It was the start and then everyone in the family started talking about their usual stuffs. It was like a third degree torture of CBI, when many people do jointly. Uncle talked about all the things I hated. How did he know my dislikes so well? Vishal was talking about the new Noddy cartoon.

I tolerated this for 15-20 minutes but when I saw no one stopping, I got up to go.

"Literature is going nowhere" Uncle said. New boring topic! Oh, I had to sit because it was ill manner to leave while someone wanted to say something. His speech changed from politics to literature.

Again I got up to leave after sometime but the same thing repeated. I got up for the third time, this time with enormous dedication and commitment. No one can make me sit this time. I went to the door, opened it but oh shit, uncle interrupted again. But this time I was outside the door but Vishal and Uncle didn't want to stop. I closed the door in hope they will stop. But Uncle again said something and I had to open the door to listen to what he was saying. Why my Nani taught me so many manners?

"When will you come next?" Vishal asked while Uncle was thinking about what to say after this.

Never, I wanted to say. "Maybe after the exams" I said.

The moment he stopped and before he could start again I banged the door real hard and ran away to the stairs. I was virtually running. From the corner of my eye I saw everyone was waving hands saying bye to me from the balcony, but I was too afraid to look back. What if they called me again to say something? I paced my feet until I reached a safe distance from the eerie house.

I bought cold-drinks to bring myself to normal state and then took the bus to go to the college, feeling like escaped prisoner of Tihar jail

There was a whole new season going in JU. Election was within a month and all the students' parties were promoting themselves at fullest extent. They wanted volunteers from first year to do their works. In return first years got entry into the party and recognition.

Apart from various faculties, there was a latent faculty-faculty of politics. In this faculty there are excellent Profs, who themselves were students a few years back. And the placement of this faculty too is excellent. The students get placed in very good local and national political parties.

Viks was hungry for power and recognition so he also joined one of the students' unions. His personality also matched with this. But we felt joining union was not a good thing as it hindered with the studies. And getting in politics, I think, can get us into troubles also. We warned him about this. But when does Viks listen to us. It was a similar situation one day when I was de-mystifying why Viks doesn't bath.

"Why don't you bath? Are you hydrophobic?" I asked him one day.

"Why do you bath? Tell me" he asked me back.

"I bath because I love water, I love cleanliness"

"What if one remains clean even without bathing? I mean you bath because you're dirty and I don't bath because I'm not dirty" he said.

"I'm not hydrophobic maybe you're hydro manic" He said after a pause. Who could argue with him now?

New Year Eve

Maybe I started liking her, but I wasn't too sure. Agreed she was beautiful, but there were prettier girls like Ishika. Was she the girl for me? She was a metro girl. But she was not like other metro girls, she had something like me. She was tender, gentle.

I couldn't meet her since last one month because of semesters but I called her daily. I bought "10 ka top up" daily. And we continued with our missed-call-study technique.

By this time Sid had taught me some Bangla. The first word which I learned was "Kaino" meaning why, and I used the word quite often whenever I talked with Sonia. But many Bangla words still confused me like "machkhane" which means centre. In Hindi this word sounds like eating fish and I thought how much these people like eating fish. Similarly the word 'ghmobo' sounds as if someone is going to roam about somewhere. And I still can't unwind the mystery that why Bengalis don't drink anything but always eat.

Last night study of Sid's Xeroxed notes, combined with some cheating was sufficient to pass the sems. We developed special cheating techniques like CHAIN REACTION and LFA(Load Fulcrum Effort). The semesters got over and I had to go home for the winter break. I came back to hostel, packed my luggage. The luggage consisted of dirtiest of the clothes, bed sheets, stinky socks, and few books to show nani that I study. I took the bus to Howrah. Howrah platform was as crammed as ever.

From the train I called Sonia. I wanted to end my full balance talking to her. The connection got cut again, but it was nice talking to Sonia. When the network was too feeble to talk I sent her as many messages as I could. Sometimes they deduct the balance afterwards.

"I'll miss you in home" I SMSed last. I always gave her hints but there was no reaction from the other side. She never showed her cards. Girls are too complicated and it's better I stay away from their complex psychology. Half an hour later I saw my balance was Rs -14.98. It gave me great satisfaction. I went to sleep, I knew after getting up I would find myself in Ranchi.

Home was enjoyable for the first week, but after that I started missing Kolkata, Viks, Yash, Sid and Sonia. Man I was missing them like anything, especially the last one. And I was gripped to come back to kolkata. I never thought that fooling my nani would be so easy. I just said that I have a project work and she never asked a question in return.

So I reached Kolkata on 30th Dec. It was 8 in the night when I reached hostel. Hostel was totally a different place. It was never so empty. I went to the terrace and called Sonia.

"Hey. How are you?"

"I'm fine. But why did you call. Your cell must be in roaming." Sonia said. She was always concerned about my expenses.

"No no it is not roaming"

"What do you mean?"

"Fool, I'm in Kolkata"

"How come you are in Kolkata? You had your winter break" Now what to tell her. Should I admit the real reason or something else? I chose the latter.

"I had some Project work"

"I'm not helping you this time. But hey! Why are you spending the New Year here? You could have come after it"

"For Profs here, new year means nothing. We have no option other than following their way"

"Are your friends also here?"

"No one is here. I will be having a lonely new year"

"If you want you can come with me. I'll go out with friends." She said. Ah! That's what I was dying for.

On 31st we went to City Center -I, Sonia and Monika.

"Hi whitie. Sorry I mean Monika" After calling someone whitie for so many days Monica didn't come to my mouth.

"What did you say just now?" Sonia's antenna cached my slip of tongue.

"I didn't say anything."

"I heard you say something some white or something"

"No I didn't"

"Rahul. Tell"

Lastly I had to give up. You can't win against two girls pulling your hairs out. I had to tell them the whole nomenclature system of ours.

"You guys are disgusting. And what was my name?" Sonia asked.

"Pinky" I said. She sighed with pseudo anger and disgust.

"Girls girls. Please stop yelling. Let's have ice-cream."

We went to the food court.

"What ice-cream will you have?" Monika asked me.

There was a large variety of ice-creams but thanks to Sonia and our Mall trips that now I knew much about these things. Sonia and I chose black current while Monika chose Blind love. We sat over the stairs with our ice-creams. There was an RJ programme going to begin here in the premises of City center on the eve of New Year.

Monica took my bag which I never brought to college, but had brought today for shopping. She took out a pen from her purse and wrote big 'R' 'S' on my bag. Then she repeatedly rubbed her pen to make R and S bold.

"Do you know what R and S stand for?" She asked.

"Rahul Sharma" I said like a dumb even when I guessed what she might mean.

"No it means..." She said and wrote 'ahul' and 'onia' in small font size after R and S respectively. She did this and started grinning

"Stop Moni" Sonia said and hit on her hand.

This was followed by FLAMES, LAKME and similar love games. This is how they played it. They keep trying different permutations of variations of names unless and until something of their interest comes. They calculated FLAMES of Sonia and Rahul and it came S, sister. She changed the names to Rahul Sharma and Sonia Bose, and it came L, love.

I didn't know whether they were giving me hints of Sonia's liking me or were just making fun of me; I knew they had figured out my inclination for her. I was afraid to reach any conclusion as girls always do like this. They will tease you like this and when you propose them they will react like – Rahul, I never thought you will do like this. I thought we were just good friends." I didn't want this to happen here and so I acted as if I couldn't see or hear anything. I was keeping myself busy watching the RJ speaking which inspired me from within. I also wanted to perform on stage. I wanted to start my own Band.

We left City Center at around 7 and returned by bus. Besides pulling bus' sponge out, we were discussing our old school crushes and our past life. It's always interesting to know one's past. She told about her crushes named Nikhil and Armaan.

"How many guys have proposed you till now?" I asked her. The number of proposals a girl has got is directly proportional to her widely accepted beauty and is a good universal scale to quantity beauty. Proposals over ten gave the girl an A rank and over fifteen an A+. I was not too amused to know that she got 14 proposals (and my proposal being fifteenth will give her A+ rank). But when asked about me, I had only one-sided crushes to tell her.

On 1st Jan, Sonia was going to Presidency College to meet her old school friend Rashmi. She asked me to go with her because Rashmi also wanted to meet me. When girl's friends want to meet you then there has to be something fishy. We went to the Presidency College to meet her.

Rashmi was puffing a cigar, lying on the ground. She was fat and tall, roughly my height(or an inch more than me) and had dense curly broom-like hair. She was wearing tight ripped jeans and a loose white T-shirt. She got up when she saw Sonia and they hugged like kumbh-mela-lost sisters.

"We are meeting after almost a year" Sonia said holding Rashmi's hand.

"So here is your Rahul" Rashmi said to Sonia. Sonia glared at her; I gave the same blank look as if I couldn't understand what she said.

"Come Rahul I'll show you my college. Sonia you stay here. Let me spend some time with this handsome" Oh! Did she really say handsome???

"See one of the most famous arts college of India. The classrooms are closed so I can't take you inside. See there is my department. Hey why are you so quiet? Say something."

"Nice college" I was feeling uncomfortable with her. I don't like girls who smoke and she was smoking continuously one after another.

"Here is your belonging. I know you must be worried about him while he was with me." She taunted when we came back. Sonia stamped her feet. I again acted as deaf and dumb.

I don't like Rashmi type of girls; I mean the outspoken and too bold type of girls.

"Can you speak Mr Rahul? You know, I don't like you for this" Rashmi said.

"What can I say? You two girls talk" I didn't want to talk to her. Her boorish personality was turning me off. She was also a member of her college union and I hated unions. She had all the ingredients I hated the most. Probably God created her considering all my dislikes.

"Ah! Thank God you said something. What should we talk of to involve you in our discussion?

"AAAh...you tell what qualities do you expect in your life partner?" from where did this question fall? I know it was something related to Sonia.

"She should be beautiful, understanding and should take care of my house and baby"

"So you want housewife?"

"No I don't want a housewife but just want her to take care of my baby"

"Now you tell Sonia, what kinda husband do you want?" Rashmi asked her.

"Looks are not important for me. All I expect is that he should be understanding and supportive"

"And" I said.

"And he should earn good and should be well mannered and should be at a reputed post and should have a decent presentable personality and he should be caring and he should take me out every weekend and he should listen to my words....".

"In short she wants a complete package? What have you left in your list?" I said interrupting her. We all laughed together at this. Girls want everything in one man.

"Don't you think the person with these qualities you are searching, is not far from you?" Rashmi said while lighting another cigar.

"Why do you smoke? Girls shouldn't smoke this much." I said mainly to change the topic.

"Why girls shouldn't smoke. When you guys do then it's okay and when we do you have problems?" Rashmi said.

"I myself don't smoke"

"What? You left it or what?" She said as if in a shock.

"I haven't even tried once"

"Oh! You little baby, what about drinks? Have you ever tasted the divine red wine?"

"I have never tried drinks too"

"How is this possible?" She said interrupting. "Even Sonia has tried drinking and smoking many times"

"Ya I have smoked and drunk 4-5 times with Rashmi" Sonia said.

"You wana try it now? Have it. It's expensive." She offered me Cigar. Spoilt girl Rashmi, spoilt Sonia also and now is trying the same with me.

"No thanks" I said. And what did she want to say telling Cigar was expensive. Can't I buy it or what? This girl was seriously getting on my nerves. I despised her.

"You remember Tomoghno?" Rashmi said to Sonia. Sonia nodded and Rashmi continued

"He is such a fucked up guy. You know what he did last week. I was in a College Union meeting. Suddenly I got his SMS that he would have sleeping pills if I don't talk to him."

"Then" Sonia asked

"Then what? As if I care. I was doing College Union's work and kept doing it."

"Who is Tomoghno by the way" I asked.

"He is my ex-boyfriend" Rashmi said.

"Then" Sonia asked.

"Then his friend called me saying Tomoghno has gulped 20 sleeping pills. He is dying. Please come to see him soon. I SMSed him Fuck Off."

"One hour later Tomoghno's SMS came that he was dying and wanted to meet me for the last time. And I said, Oh my God, you haven't still died after taking twenty sleeping pills" And Rashmi and Sonia laughed and chortled at this.

I was feeling uneasy and suffocated hearing all this and I decided to leave and told them that I wasn't feeling well.

"From Sealdah you can take direct local train to Jadavpur. It is not far" Rashmi gave directions to me as I left. Sonia decided to spend some time with her long parted friend.

"You know Tomoghno was good only on bed, rest of the time he was a big asshole." I heard this much till I got out of the audible range.

"Jadavpur?" I asked a passenger standing in the train and he nodded in affirmation. Although there was no space left, I tried to get up on the train. Oh! The floor was packed. With me half-hanging, the train started.

"Uncle please let me enter. This is my first time in local train. I can't continue hanging." I said to a fellow passenger. He was kind and pulled me inside. But there were forces from other bodies also and the action reaction pairs pushed me deep inside, far away from the gate.

The first stoppage came. Atleast a hundred people rushed inside. I almost lost my control which I somehow retained holding a rod. I revolved inside as if I were in the centre of a whirlpool. Meanwhile my spectacles fell on the floor. The problem with blinds like us is that even to search specs we need specs. I got down and dug my hand between the feet and found something like the glass of my specs. I dug further in to find the rest of it. But Alas! It was into bits and pieces, including the other glass. And without glasses I was virtually blind.

The second stoppage came and then the third and then the stoppage I was waiting for-Jadavpur. I used my full energy to cross the crowd to get near the gate, as the train slowed down. Two buttons of my shirt got plucked as I managed to reach the gate. I only had to get down now. But crowd flowing inside the train pushed me crushingly to the centre of the train again. And the train started. I waved a small bye to Jadavpur, what else could I do?

I couldn't get down before Sonarpur, four stops after Jadavpur, being completely blind. I had only a piece of cracked glass to see this world, the platform, bus no. Somehow I took a bus and swore that I'd never get into local train ever again in my life.

At night I was lying down on my bed. I have a habit which I don't know is good or bad, that, whatever haunts my mind, I type it in my mobile and save it in drafts, so that I can forget about it for the time being and unburden my brain and think about it later. The thing that was haunting me was that Sonia had tried smoking and drinking and she had friends like Rashmi. Okay in metro culture these things are normal, but was it just smoking or drinking or more than that? And I was thinking about the Tamoghno and Rashmi thing too. And suddenly cold water ran through my spine. I typed what I had in my mind. "*vergin*?"

Don't know when I slept but a beep in my mobile woke me up. Still half asleep I saw the screen of the mobile "Message delivered: Sonia"

My sleep sublimated Shit!!! What should I do now? Switch off the mobile? Throw it? And what if she calls me back and scolds me? I asked a girl about this thing, which no one should ever ask. And other faculty of my mind was busy thinking, what if her reply came 'no'?

My SMS tone beeped and I jumped to open the SMS. I closed my eyes tightly and murmured a small prayer and when I opened I saw "Yes I'm. What about you? And the spelling is virgin"

"Of course I'm. I don't even know the spelling" I replied smartly.

Now again my mind was full of questions: Why didn't she get angry at such a question? Why did she ask about my virginity in return? Was she also interested in me?

Meanwhile I and Sonia had newly discovered a place for hangout, behind Pharma Ceutical Building or PCB, as we called it. We started meeting there regularly. We sat under our favourite tree, demonstrating JU's tradition of hanging out in *gachtola*.

I was still testing whether she had something for me or not. And I was to check this by a new theory developed by Yash, the arm theory. I kept my arm on her shoulder slowly and acted as if I kept it unconsciously. And I didn't move my arm off her for the next five minutes and then asked her "Is my arm heavy?"

And she said "No. It's ok?"

Yuhu. She was allowing me to keep my arm on her. Crackers were bursting inside my mind. And the crackers soon got converted into whistle. Not my whistle but a guard's whistle.

"What are you both doing here? It is seven and you both are still sitting here. Don't you have your homes you shameless people? Should I complain about you? Get off now you two." The guard asked.

"These people don't have any work." Sonia said clinching her teeth, picked her bag and hit the floor hard and walked briskly.

We Indians are hypocrite in the matter of love. In India love is a topic in which only theory class takes place. I was just sitting with Sonia and wasn't doing anything other than keeping my arm on her shoulder. I feel they are jealous. These losers never got any girlfriend when they were young and so they're jealous seeing others'.

But the thing to think about was why did she get so much angry? Did she also like it?

19th Jan

I and Yash were sitting in BBC-Basket Ball Court. This was because second half was boycott., implying holiday for that day. Sid rushed away to home for studying. In JU we got several free holidays because of boycotts and deputations - sometimes of students' union, sometimes of teachers' union, sometimes of staffs' union and sometimes because of Bengal bandh. We were used to the deputations and boycotts since the last month; they were very frequent because of Nandigram issue. Viks had also participated in the deputation with the union. This was a big matter and various other colleges' unions were also participating for the cause.

"Where are you? What are you doing now? My classes for today are over." I SMSed Sonia. This was the usual SMS which I used to send. The language was suitably chosen to hide my intensive desire to meet her, but just to make a small indication. I wanted her to invite me.

"My class is off too. Come over the construction place" Her SMS came, inviting me to meet up.

We were meeting like this almost every day since this New Year. We walked to every corners, from Kashmir to Kanyakumari of JU. We explored various do-not-disturb hangout places for us to sit and talk. But we avoided Jheel Paar, as it was the place mostly for 'professional' boyfriends-girlfriends. Yes! They were boyfriends and girlfriends by profession and they changed their jobs every two months to a company generally better in prospects. They were really seasoned in everything, from good to bad. This place was also (in)famous due to its savana grasslands, behind which the professionals did their jobs. Guards often gave income tax raids in the place, sometimes to increase their income.

"Going where?" Yash asked.

"Where else" I replied.

"When will you propose her?"

"I don't know" I said.

I met Sonia at the Construction place, the place which became a famous hangout place right from the day its construction started. Now even when it was fully constructed it had to carry its name. From there we went to PCB.

"What is your favourite colour?" She asked. Why is she asking me my favourites suddenly? Was she matching our compatibility? Everything she did nowadays created doubts in my mind.

"Blue, but why?" I replied.

"Just like this. What's your favourite cuisine?" She asked.

"Chinese. Especially Chow-mein" I said.

"What's your favourite movie?" She asked again now playing with other strand of hair.

"Titanic" I replied. I don't like someone questioning too much but this time it was okay as it was safer to play at the back foot.

"Wow! We're so much similar" She said with sparkle in her eyes. As far as Titanic was concerned half the world has Titanic their favourite movie.

"What's your idea of dream house? Mine is on seashore." she asked again playing with her hair. Girls love doing it, and so do we (not with our hair though).

"Me too" I replied. Well I would prefer house on mountains, but a house on seashore was also okay for me. And why lose the chance of creating one more similarity between us.

"Do you like to get up in the morning or you're a night person?" she said. Now, over with her hair, she was gazing at her polished nails. It was some silvery shade of blue and was looking sexy. She was rotating her fist at different angles and her nails were sparkling.

"I hate waking early. I love sleeping" I said scratching my head and yawning. The mention of sleep made me sleepy.

"I also love sleeping. Given me a chance I would sleep the entire day." She said. Her eyes were now at the nails of her feet which were buffed with the nail polish of same colour.

"Me too" I replied. I was thinking if we got married, it would be so good for us if we both slept more. More sleep and longer fun hours.

"Hey it's strange. Again same" What was strange in this? Most of the questions were too common.

She was asking me more questions and I followed "me too" policy.

"We're very much similar. Aren't we? I hadn't had such a similarity with anyone before." She said.

I again replied with my favourite two words "me too".

"I think you're copying me." I said after a pause.

"No. You are copying me, you're copy cat."

"No you're copy cat"

"You're copy cat, copy rat, Xerox machine"

"And you. You're copy lizard" "Sonia is a lizard. Copy lizard. Na na na na" I said and she flared her nose.

"Hey jokes apart, tell me, who do you like more, Mom or Dad?" This time I asked her a question. I had something hidden inside me.

"Mom."

"Why mom? Generally girls like their dads more." I asked. I sensed something.

"No but I like my mom more and don't like my dad"

"Don't like?" More doubts popped in my mind.

"Leave it. Talk about something else" She said with her mood clearly off. Her face was now a bit tensed.

I could feel what she might be feeling because maybe I was also facing the same situation. I gave it a thought. Should I tell her about my deepest secret? I had never told anyone about this before. How will she react? Anyways I'll had to tell her some day or other, then why not today?

"You know something. One important thing that I never told you was that my parents are divorced and separated" I said.

"What?" She said with her eye-brows up and blinking eyes giving a really surprised expression.

"The same is my story. My parents are also divorced and I live with my mom. I have no contacts with my dad."

"What?" I said almost taken aback, little happy little amused. Now this was not a created similarity. It was the epitome of similarity now.

"I don't live with either of my parents. My nani keeps me."

Two divorced families' children have so many sorrows to share, which they can't share with anyone else. We talked about how and what happened and how we felt.

"Dad never loved me. When I was in class 5, I got malaria. I was very ill. I was lying on the bed. My mom told him to get medicines for me. And you know what he said?" Sonia was saying.

"What?"

"He said I don't care if she lives or dies. Let her die. I don't know why he hates me this much." She said with her face fire hot.

"Hey Sonia. Relax." I said clasping her hand.

"But you I felt very relaxed after telling this to you. I haven't told this to anyone, not even to Rashmi."

I was back with my "Me too". To whom will I say these things. These things are buried deep inside us. I didn't know why I was also happy.

"Anyways, I've to leave now. I've my German class at RKM" She said getting up and shedding off the dust of floor from her jeans. She had joined German language class at Ram Krishna Mission Institute of Culture at Gariahat last week.

Before this day I wasn't too sure about proposing, but today, I was too much impressed, almost carried away by the similarities. I became sure Sonia was the right girl for me. Ya we had different cultures, she was a metro girl, but she had a traditional touch. And that similarity, you don't find with everyone; and we shared common anguish and soreness.

I saw in my cell, it was 19th January, Friday. Next two days were Saturday and Sunday barrier, coz she didn't come to college on weekends. It was impossible for me to wait for two more days. I wanted to upgrade our friendship status to relationship one. I wanted Sonia to be my girlfriend.

As we were getting out of gate no. 4, I recollected all the tips and tricks Yash gave about proposing. "Do it with a red rose...Look into her eyes and say confidently I Love you....confidence is all the girls look for...etc etc..."

Although I firmly believed in Yash's ideas, I was too nervous to execute them. Somewhere inside me, I felt that proposing was nothing more than a formality. Her friends pointed about it and I passed the shoulder test.

But even after all this I was nervous like anything. What if she says no? Forget relation, I'd lose her even as friend. And I didn't want to lose her now. My hands and legs froze and my confidence shattered.

"Can I ask you a question?" I asked looking forty-five degrees away from her, not looking into her eyes. Those big eyes made me frightened.

"Ask."

I started walking to and fro in one metre range. Walking reduces tension and boosts your thinking power-I read somewhere.

"I'm getting late. Tell fast. And why are you walking" Sonia said.

"Ya ya I'm. Wait a bit."

One auto was passing. She waved hand to the auto and it stopped.

"Tell it tomorrow" She said while going towards the auto.

"No No No. Please wait. Just wait till the next auto comes."

I told auto driver to go. He gave me I-will-eat-you look.

"Say fast. I'm getting late."

I sighed before saying "I don't know about you, but I like you". I said in one breath. Saying at one go is the easiest option.

"Like? Like in what sense?" She asked. By this time my BP was high enough to burst my arteries and veins. "In every sense" I said, myself not understanding what I was saying. My mind was choked. I was about to faint. I never felt like this before. Love can give you extremes of the feelings.

She started laughing. Just after that an auto arrived and she sat in that auto.

"Hey! What's your reply?" I shouted.

She didn't say anything and continued grinning.

What did the laughter mean? Did it mean she was happy that I proposed her finally? Or she took my proposal very lightly like many losers proposing her?

"One New message received" Showed my mobile screen.

My heart started thumping as it wanted to come out of my body. Whose message was it? What was inside the message? I pressed the button to open the message. But oh no! It hanged. I hit the mobile hard into my other hand.

Shit! When I had to see the result of my first proposal it hanged. Who made this bloody mobile? I opened the back of mobile and took the battery and SIM out and then placed them back into my cell. But after that also the cell didn't get on. I started biting my nails till all my nails ended up. I wished I had more nails to bite.

Was the SMS too shocking for the mobile that it hanged? Will it be equally shocking for me too?

I rushed to Yash's flat. He had several spare phones.

"Yash. Please give me a cellphone" I said panting.

"But why?"

"Sonia...propose...SMS" I was getting out of breath because of running.

He gave me a phone and I inserted my SIM and when I switched it on the SMS showed "Yes. I do"

Yash also peeped on the screen and blowed a loud whistle. I sighed with relief and happiness. Meanwhile Viks also came there.

"PARTY" He shouted when He heard about this. Yes, it was worth a party. But I knew, Viks was only interested in food.

We went to BANJARA our favourite restaurant near the hostel. This restaurant shared every joys and sorrows right from birthday treats to placement treats to proposal treat.

"How you did it?" Yash asked.

"In my own style" I said. I was the hero for the night. Why should I tell them that I almost fainted and ruin my image?

Although I completely hated it, this weekend again, I had to go to Dum Dum; the only reason being my nani. She had been my only guardian since the past six years, after my mom and dad left each other, and me. And when she compelled me to come here I couldn't say no to her.

This time the milieu was somewhat different as I reached there. Uncle, aunty and Vishal were sitting together and some hot discussion was going on.

"Rahul! Come beta. See your brother doesn't study well for his boards" Aunty said when I was opening my shoes.

"Study son. Your boards are not too far" Uncle said to Vishal.

"You should devote more hours to study. We want you to pass this time" Aunty said.

"You tell him Rahul beta. Is this the way a tenth class student should study?" I was being pulled into the discussion which I didn't want.

"I'm coming after drinking water" I said and went to the kitchen to fetch water. I hid behind the door and peeped from the keyhole. And hearing them was as easy as fetching water from sea as their multi-decibels could be heard easily even at one kilometre distance.

"We give you the best facilities to you. You get every book you want. We have arranged you tuitions for each subject. Can't we expect good marks in return?" Aunty said.

"But I study 5-6 hours daily" Vishal tried to defend.

"You don't study. You just sit idly with the books." Uncle said.

This lecture was going on. I saw Vishal's fire igniting and suddenly the sound bomb exploded "Why do you tell this to me every day? I'm bored of listening the same long lectures every day."

"See how this failure is shouting. A twice tenth failed spoiled brat." Uncle's voice was also rising.

Hey! I was to encounter the sight of the family dramas live (and free!!!). The "Battle Of Dum Dum" was about to begin. I checked my position so that I could keep myself safe and sound. The team was decided as you see; it was uncle and aunty Vs Vishal. All the three warriors took their stands.

"Papa" Vishal screamed. It was like whistle to start the war. Soon this shout-a-loud virus spread to other members also.

"Mummy, you tell me to study but nani told me you also failed tenth twice" Vishal to aunty.

"You said this to your mother, beta?" Aunty came with her K-series mother's emotional dialogues. Atleast these serials serve some purpose, teaching Indian women good dialogues.

"I don't need books. I don't want to study" Vishal tossed the book up in the air.

"You are shameless" She threw tomato on Vishal. She was cutting vegetables.

Vishal saved himself from Aunty's hand grenade.

"You don't study and waste our money. And you waste hankies also. You lose one hanky daily in your school and steal other hankies from my cupboard" Aunty said

"Oh! Here is the pick-pocket of my hankies too. Do you know how much embarrassing it feels in the office without hankies?" Uncle fired. He shouted so loud that the building started shaking.

The cause of fight was changed now from studies to hankies. Vishal tore a pillow out of anger which created smoke bomb effect. Cotton and feathers were sinking slowly from air to ground.

For the next half an hour the skirmish continued with the cause constantly changing from hankies to maggy to socks to many things.

As the war ended, the floor looked like big dustbin with cotton, feathers and pages spread here and there and the red spots of tomatoes on the walls symbolizing the bloodshed.

This was the end to the WWE-home edition. Excellent show I must say, complete entertainment. I wanted to clap and whistle at the end of the show and congratulate the whole family but somehow curbed my desire.

First Official Date

Five days after proposing her, we were talking over the phone. I asked "Hey, what is date?"

"Meeting and all is dating" She replied.

"So we are dating everyday? Even before I proposed you?", I asked.

"Ya, Sort of"

"But I thought dating was something like both boy and girl going out together, watching movies, visiting different places, walking and talking etc etc"...(etc meant kiss which I didn't say out of hesitation), I was saying this from my experiences from TV and movies.

"And I want a date like that, so when are we going?" I said in one go.

She started laughing. Can anyone explain what was the point in laughing now? Girls laugh and cry for no reasons.

"How about tomorrow?" I asked in somewhat agitated tone.

I termed this date as our FIRST OFFICIAL DATE, because:-

(a) Now we were declared as boyfriend and girlfriend. It was not like those pre-relational times when Monika or Rashmi taunted.

(b) It was the first time after proposing her that we were going outside JU. And this was going to be the thing, what I knew as date.

She was standing with her folded hands when I came to JU. She was wearing white top and black jeans. And today she wore an 8 shaped ear-ring which looked very mysterious. And she applied light lipstick of pink colour which matched fully with her lips and made it glitter. And her perfume, oh! I'm always a big fan of her choice of perfumes. What great scent she uses, which always makes me mad.

"You are always late" She said pointing at her wristwatch.

I raised my palms in a gesture saying both what I can do and sorry.

"So, where are we going today?" I asked.

"I don't know. You say." she shrugged.

"This is absurd, you are a localite, you must be knowing about all the places of Kolkata, so you should be the one who should be deciding"

"I don't know, my brain is not working. You think and say if you want to go somewhere, or else college is not a bad place"

"What??College Again!!! Are you mad?? We roam around in the college everyday. C'mon this is supposed to be our first official date and we decided to go somewhere, now please don't do like this, apply your brain and decide a place where we are going"

"How about THE NEW MALL? Have you ever been there before?"

"Good idea! I've never been there"

"Alright then, let's go. But I have one condition. See I have my German class today at 6.30 in RKM and I don't want to miss it. So we must come back by 6. Is it okay?"

"Yes sweetheart" For the first time I was calling her sweetheart, using the new rights I got being a boyfriend. But frankly speaking I don't like the terms boyfriends and girlfriends, I prefer calling ourselves lovers.

"Hey. This is my first date and I am nervous" I said in an anxious tone breaking the silence. She peeped into my face smiled and then burst into laughter. Again this was outlandish why she was laughing. Meanwhile I noticed her snow-white cheeks turned pink and she was looking so cute, so gorgeous.

"You are so cute" she said pulling my cheeks.

We got out from gate and crossed the road to take auto. It was strange in our relationship that the girl decided the place, route etc, as if she were taking me on date. I am a complete waste because even being in second semester; I wasn't that familiar with most of Kolkata. There are thousands of bus running and it is really easy for me to get confused and take the wrong route. And also because I've a very bad memory about roads and routes. I wondered how people remember it. I was thinking when I'll have a car after 3-4 years and will have to drive it on my own, how will I remember all the roads, the turnings? And driving with family will mean more responsibility. What if I get confused and get lost? Will I have to keep a driver? Can't I remember roads?

This is what happens to you when you are on your first date. Your mind wanders randomly, generally thinking of past and future.

"Get down. It's Gariahat", she said breaking my dreams. From there we had to walk for 5 minutes. She told me to "walk separately as if we are not together. My nani resides in that locality and if anyone sees me with you then I could be in trouble."

See this is the problem with local girls; they can't go here because her nanis lives here and there. It was damn irritating. I start thinking why are they restricting new love birds? Weren't they young ever, say 40-50 years back. Anyways I got separated from her, although I didn't want. When you have a one week new girlfriend you feel like staying together for 24 hours a day with her.

"Nothing is too special in this mall I guess. I expected a bit more from this place." I said as we reached the New Mall.

"Ya, this is nothing as compared to city center or Inox forum" She said.

"Oh Shit. Let's get out of here as soon as possible" She said looking left and right, somewhat worried.

"Now what happened?" I asked.

"My mama is also here with his family. Let's go. The mall is not that good and I also don't want to be caught by any relative."

"You and your relatives"

"Anyways can you wait for 1 minute? May I go to drink water ma'am?" I said pointing towards the water cooler cum purifier. She nodded in reply.

There was no glass. What a shoddy mall. I opened the tap and got down to drink water with my palms. I took the first sip in my mouth.

"OAAAAAAA..........THU....THU........AWAAAAAAAAH" Was my reaction while I spitted water.

"Hey the water is extremely salty" I said. Water was here and there, everywhere in 2 metre range from me. Meanwhile a lady staff came there and gave me a very dirty look. She opened her mouth to say something but we escaped in nanoseconds from the backdoor.

"Horrible! Seriously horrible. Let's go somewhere else"

"Now where? You decide now. My brain is not working"

"What? Again you are doing like this! Is your brain is a trolley which needs to be pushed everytime?"

"How about Inox forum?"

"That will be a great idea."

"We will have to take auto from here. Then bus number E-1"

"Let's go in taxi"

"Taxi. No it would be very expensive."

"You don't have to worry so much"

"You go by taxi and I'm not with you"

Anyways , We reached Inox Forum Mall.

"Let's go to the food counter straightaway."I said because my hunger was on its extreme. Luckily we got a corner table. I had no clue what had happened to my luck which had bugged me always. I ordered the food and sat on our seat.

"Remember last time we came here on your birthday" I made her remember.

"Ya. Early days" she said. We sat close to each other on the corner table. I was holding her soft and warm hand.

"Sit a little far. People are looking at us and there are many people who will throw their objections"

"I don't care. I'm sitting with my girlfriend and I'm paying (read overpaying) for the place and food then what problem they are having."

"No" She took my hand off her finally and pushed my chair. I don't know why girls care about their surrounding so much. Why are they so much afraid of strangers' comments that have nothing to do with us?

Half an hour later we had our food finished but I didn't want to leave the romantic place so early. You don't get corner seat every day afterall. To pass time I brought some cold-drinks because it was the cheapest thing one could get there. We had 3 rounds of cold-drinks to spend 1.5 hour there.

"We should get out of here or else they will throw us out", she said.

"Its just 3.30 now, where will we be going now?"

"I don't know just leave this place now" we got out and then I repeated my question

"Where next?"

"I don't know, You say"

"I don't know is your patent dialogue I guess! ", I said in irritated tone.

"Uff....Do you want to see my school? It is at a walking distance from here."

"Sure", I said.

While walking to her school I was imagining her in blue and white school dress. How cute she must be looking in her school dress. Girls look much sexier in uniform. What if I had met when I was in my school? What if she was in my class? What if she was my childhood friend?

"This is my school", she said breaking my dream again. She always did this.

"Wow! Beautiful buildings. Can we go inside and see the classrooms", I said.

"Oh My God! Miss Sujata is coming out. What time it is? 3.45. Oh shit! This is the time when school gets over. Leave this place now. Just now" She was uttering non-stop.

"You have problem everywhere. Can we go somewhere where you

don't have problems?"

"I decided last two places. Now you decide."

"You are simply horrible. How far is the Birla Planetarium?"

"Not too far. 15 minutes walking from here"

"Let's go then"

There was a TV shop in our way and I saw a glimpse from the corner of my eye.

"Hey! It was India Vs Pakistan today. Can we stay here for 2 minutes?"

"You guys and your cricket matches!"

The 2 minutes soon got converted into 15 minutes.

"Are you coming or should I go home?"

"No, I'm coming, just two balls. Let Shoaib's over get completed"

"Enough! I'm going. Bye"

"No. Please don't. Can't you wait for 1 more ball?"

"Get lost!" she shouted and she started walking. I watched the last ball and then started following her.

"Don't talk to me"

"I'm sorry"

"You love cricket and don't love me"

This sounded strange. Why do girls compare themselves to anything as silly as a game? But I didn't try to think about it. Girls think in a different way and burning our brains to understand them will be a total time and energy waste.

"Hey! I love you", paused and the said "more than anything else"

"I love you" this time a bit louder. Loud enough to make people notice us.

"Are you idiot? Will you stop this now?" She said with anger partly vanished due to the publically declared I Love You.

"Who started it?"

BIRLA PLANETARIUM showed the board. As we went inside to buy the ticket we looked at the show timings

5:00 PM – English (30 mins)

5:30 PM – Bangla (30 mins)

6:00 PM – Hindi (30 mins)

"What time is it? 5:05. Oh shit! We missed the English show by 5 minutes. All because of you and your match."

"I said sorry for it na. Now please stop this and get tickets for the Bangla show"

"What? Are you in your senses Mr Rahul? Will you watch Bangla show?"

"Why to worry when I have a translator with me"

"But I think it will be too late at the end of the show and I don't want to miss my RKM class at any cost"

"Don't worry so much, we will reach before time. It's my guarantee."

"If my class gets missed I'll kill you"

We entered the dark room of planetarium. I chose the last seat explaining her "this will be the best place to see the stars." Actually I was talking of different stars ;-) . Actually the whole Birla Planetarium idea was my plan. Show started, lights got off and our show begun. I held her hand and planted a kiss on her cheek. Her cheek smelt so sweet like some fruit. I kissed it again and again. I didn't go beyond that because I didn't want to make any bad impression on our first official date.

"See this constellation" suddenly the light intensity got high and everything became visible. I turned my head in a flash. Light levels got low again and we resumed to have fun again. The show ended soon and so did our show. I hoped the show could last a bit longer.

"See what time it is! 6:10" she shouted while coming out from the planetarium.

"Don't worry 20 minutes would be sufficient to reach there if we take a taxi"

In the taxi, I was thinking this was the end of our date. She will go to her German class and I'll return hostel. This date was going to get over in a few minutes. My mood was getting dismal now. I hoped I could be with her a little longer.

"See the road jam! That Bangla show idea was totally crap."

"Really? I thought it was fun"

As the road got a bit clear we asked the taxi to drive a little faster.

The moment we reached RKM, she started yelling "6:45.See the time. See"

"Yes" I said from inside but from outside I made a sorry face.

"Anyways I can't get into class now. And if I go home now, your mom will doubt so much."

"That means you have to spend 1.5 more hours with me."

"No other option"

"Let's go to CCD then" I said as Gariahat was our area and I knew this place fully, an exception. Though the CCD was getting hard on my pocket now but this was my first official date afterall. I wanted to make it grand.

In the CCD went there had coffee and chatted for half an hour.

"I'll pay for it. You've spend too much today." She said.

"No. I'll pay. You don't have to worry about me"

"Keep your mouth shut. I won't let you do this" She was too unbending and she paid the money finally and I couldn't do anything.

For the next one hour we walked from Golpark to Rashbehari. We chatted and shared our secrets. Most of our lines started with "You know what..."

After that she left for her house and I came back to the hostel.

On the way to the hostel, I SMSed her "See the left chain of your bag. Sorry, I don't like my girlfriend spending when I'm there" I put the money in her bag while she was busy paying in CCD.

It was the end of our long, exhausting but amusing, pleasurable and great "First Official Date"

Lab I Hate U

The Professor entered the class. He was an over-aged Prof, looked like just survived after his second heart attack and third could come any moment.

"Respond to your roll nos." The Prof said after coughing.

Prof said.

"Roll 1"

"Present sir" Debtanu said.

"Roll 2"

"Present sir" Arnab said.

"Why don't they give a holiday on valentine's day? There should be one." I said to Yash.

"Point, Boss! We should fight for the cause. Make deputations and strike for it. Union will also support, I guess" Viks joked smilingly.

"Roll 18"

"Roll 18"

"Roll 18"

"Yes sir" I said hastening. I was the culprit roll 18. He gave me a disgusted look from his telescopes.

I was in the class just physically, my mind and soul was with Sonia. Oh! Even on Valentines' day I was here. I could have bunked the class but seniors told that the Prof was really strict for attendance.

The class began. He wrote some alpha, beta, gamma things. I decided to take a nap. I told Viks. Who was sitting in front of me, to cover me and wake when Professor comes.

I slept calmly for fifteen minutes after which some sound broke my sleep.It was some caprice or some seriously jarring ringtone. The Prof took out his cellphone from a very pricey leather bag which was definitely costlier than his nokia-1100.

"I'm extremely sorry that your time got wasted. Don't worry I'll make it up" Prof said when he entered the class after 15 minutes.

"No" Whole class shouted but the Prof's face was reaction-less and he continued with his lecture.

This time Viks decided to sleep and asked me to monitor. The professor sincerely extended class for 20 minutes. Don't know what satisfaction they got by doing this. May be they were too afraid for leaving things for tomorrow.

And the worse thing happened when they start giving lectures on fitness, life, and other philosophical things. If it happens at the time of class it is still acceptable but when they continue this 20 minutes after class I just feel like howling.

The Prof said "I've found the best way to start the day it is to exercise for five minutes, take a deep breath of air and then finish with a cold shower. Then you feel rosy all over"

"Tell us more about Rosy" Viks said in his sleepy voice. The prof couldn't listen this with his weak ears. Anyways he left the class after five minutes.

Already 25 minutes late we entered the lab. And there was no question of bunking lab as it counted non-renewable 10 marks.

"Whr r u darling. I'm waitin 4 u. Cum fast. Love u." Her SMS started coming. She was waiting for me. We had planned for the whole day in advance.

"Hey Mermaid. I hv my lab nw. Cnt bunk it.Wil do it fast and cum in an hour. Love u." I replied back.

We had this machining lab which I thought I could finish in an hour. This was our incomplete job of last class. Only tapering and parting was left in the job. Higher depth of cut would do the things faster for us on lathe, I thought.

"Waiting 4 U." Another SMS came after an hour.

"Just 15 mre mins" I replied. By this time the tapering operation was completed and we had to do only parting. We fit the parting tool on the lathe and started parting.

"Don't give high cross feed. The tool may break" The lab instructor said. In the labs, lab instructor or LI is the head. Though Prof gave us marks but the lab instructors imparted us all the practical knowledge. Most of them have great practical experience and are very helpful and kind.

But I rotated the cross feed handle at higher speed and suddenly there was a clamour and sparks and something broke and flew off the machine. I quickly turned the lathe off, as well my eyes.

The lab instructors came to us. I saw half of my job was inside the chuck of the lathe and other half was a metre away on ground and the tool was into three pieces.

"I told you to give small feed. See now what happened" One of them said scolding though with kindness and showing concern.

"Sorry Sir" I said.

"Thank God that it didn't hurt you. I've seen many accidents happen. Your luck saved you from injury. The broken job could have filed anywhere, on your body or into your eyes." Another LI said

"We're sorry Sir" Viks said.

"Take care from the next time. Take a new job" LI continued.

"But Sir our job was almost complete" Viks defended.

He took our two-pieced job into his hands. Even the mild steel job was distorted with the impact as if the lathe had chewed it. "You will have to make a new one. You can't submit this. This is a damaged piece"

"But Sir we did all the operations, it was only the last thing which destroyed our job. You have seen us doing the whole thing" I said defending.

"Sorry I can't help it. Ask your Professor"

"Sir can we do it some other day. We can't complete it in a day."

"Professor can give you permission for that, I can't. Today is the last day of submission. Ask him if he could give you a leniency"

We knew going to Prof was wastage of time. We had to start from scratch again.

"It's been half an hour. Come na"

"Problem in lab. Will come after 1 hour" I SMSed back.

"No. Pls come fast. Waiting 4 U."

This time we were doing our work slowly and it took us more

time doing the work with less depth of cut and feed, plus I had to reply to Sonia's SMS every fifteen minutes.

"I'll cry now. Come just now. I'm alone now. Every frnd left."

"Just 15 more mins"

I knew it would take more than an hour, but I told her 15 minutes to keep her composed.

"15 minutes over. Where r u?"

"Last 15 mins"

"? :- (" She replied.

It was 6:30 when I finally submitted the job. Viks left for the hostel and I straight to the PCB.

I was imagining her face. It must be looking like burning coal or 1000 watt bulb. Her hair must be standing as after a 440 V shock. Waiting for FIVE big hours, man it was something. I remember the last time I came 10 minutes late; I had to tell her Sorry for 30 minutes. So in the ratio of 3:1 I will have to say sorry for 5x3 = 15 hours. One thing which was coming to my mouth was "I'm dead"

"Hey I'm sorry. It was none of my faults. The professor extended class and then in labs the job broke and then....."

"5 hours 4 minutes and 24 seconds. Know how much is it?"

"Ya I know it's very large amount of time. But try to understand."

"What understand? You know it's Valentine's day today. Where is my gift?"

"Ya that I have brought"

"These boring chocolates again. I expected something special on this special day." Strangely she was calm and composed and not angry. I was mystified. Even her hairs were not standing.

"First tell me how come you're not angry? I thought you would be angry with me for making you wait so long, but you don't seem so"

"I can wait whole life for you. What was the big deal in a few hours?"

"Someday I'll also make you wait for me too and then I'll see how much you wait" She continued.

"I'll wait for ages. Where is my gift by the way?"

"I have very special gift for you. Come with me"

She walked and I followed her. She took me to a corner-place. Behind the buildings, it was a place where no one came, except love birds like us. Our college is big enough to have many spots which are generally undiscovered by other people. Totally deserted, where no one could come-the perfect lovers' spot.

Suddenly she disappeared in the dark.

"Sonia. Where are you?"

"I'm here. Search me."

When I walked a little further into the bushes, someone held me from the back and bit my left ear softly. I turned back and she kissed my cheeks. We kissed and kissed and kissed. She was looking so beautiful, so gentle. We both came closer and then moved our face to kiss each other. But this time her big nose came in between. Our noses collided. I kissed her nose after that and continued to explore her further.

V-day can be the best day to give you relation a new turn, girls are in superb mood!!! Obviously we didn't do the ultimate thing but still whatever happened today was far beyond my expectations.

I returned to hostel at 8:30. Viks and Yash were waiting for me at the entrance of our room.

"How was your Valentine's day?" Viks asked

"It was nice." I said.

"What did you do?" Viks asked.

"We chatted and went to restaurant" I answered

"Come to the point. Did you kiss her?" Yash asked and I was in a dilemma weather to tell it or not. But if I don't tell anything, it would create more doubts.

"Ya" I said nodding my head.

"Liplock?" was Yash's instant excited reaction.

"Ya. Sort of" I said. I learnt this from Sonia that whenever in confusion use the word 'sort of' and you'll always be in safe side.

"Was it French Kiss?"

"I don't know what is French Kiss"

"What else did you do?" Yash asked.

"Nothing more. Just the kiss. Is it less?"

Well I did much more than that they couldn't have imagined. They were still thinking that I've achieved something.

"How did you start?" Yash asked.

"Well it started a bit strangely. We were sitting over....."

As you know the whole story was fake and I cooked up randomly the whole new story. Strangely, it was so easy to fool them including an encyclopaedia like Yash.

"Tere Bin" My cell started ringing. I had set this mp3 ringtone exclusively for Sonia. I picked up the call.

"Hello. What are you doing?" I said. A great conversation starter. Generally when you are talking to girlfriends you need topics, coz you have to talk for very long. Asking what what the other person is doing gives us some topics.

"Nothing" She replied. She always did nothing. I still think how to do this nothing.

"What else except nothing"

"Watching VH-1. Listening to Nickelback's Animals. Have you heard this song?"

"No."

"You don't listen English songs that much na?"

It was true, I didn't listen English songs. I preferred Bollywood songs. In English songs I had the vocabulary of 15-20 songs like Barbie Girl, Titanic song, Who let the dogs out, Brazil etc. At this moment I felt outdated.

We talked for another half an hour and then we kept the phone. I saw on the display of the cell "call ended 38:01" I don't know why girls always cut the call at 01 seconds. I wished I could use the pulse till 59 seconds before cutting the call.

Yash and I were sitting at the construction place one Saturday. The ambience of this place was worth watching during evenings. All the guitarists and singers sang, some played mouth organs and some flute and other musical instruments. They made perfect romantic musical evening for couples who sat there. I also sat with Sonia here but when she left I used to practice with Yash. And on weekends we devoted our full time to music since the last two months. Yash wanted to attract girls over here and moreover we wanted to get noticed by other people also. Sanskriti was just two weeks away and we didn't form a band yet. Actually it's always difficult to form a new band.

"Hey what about our band? You still want to perform in Sanskriti?"

I asked Yash when he was busy playing the tune of Hotel California.

"But we don't have any drummer and key-board player with us. We can't do it all with my guitar and your throat"

"Ya we have to look for them fast. Sanskriti is just two weeks away" He said and tuned the strings of the guitar. After that he played the chords of Summer Of 69 followed by "woh lamhe" of jal band.

He played these tunes really well and we did get noticed by a few girls and guys. We felt good and played the famous tune of Iron Maiden's Dance of death.

"Which department you?" A voice came from behind.

"Automobile and you" I said turning back towards him

"Pharmaceutical, I'm Rajeev. Which band do you play for? What's your name?"

"I'm Yash. I played in my school band. But here no band yet." Yash said.

"You play nice. We are NIGHT ROCKERS. We need a guitarist. What else can you play?"

"I can play almost everything on Spanish guitar. I'm playing since I was 7. And I remember the chords of most of the English and Hindi numbers"

"Good. Then come join us tomorrow. We'll be having a practice session at my house. Take my number. You will come na?"

"Yes why not!" We nodded. But he was calling only Yash and not me.

"Rajeev, he is Rahul, he is a singer" Yash pointed towards me.

"We have our singer, but anyways you may also come" He said just half heartedly.

Sometimes luck comes walking to you and you can't get it how?

Next day we reached Rajeev's home. He was a drummer and had the complete drum set in his house. I tried my hands on the drums and hit the drums with the stick. Among the musical instruments I like drum the most. It brings into songs a different feeling, a different tempo.

Partho came after half an hour. He was the keyboard player. Raghu also came, who was the singer.

"So here we are. You all know each other now. Here we are to form our new band" Rajeev announced.

"New band? I thought he already had a band" Yash said to me. So these guys were also amateur and had just started the band. Smile came to my mind when I retrospected that with what confidence Rajeev told me "we are Night Rockers". As if it was some Linkin Park or something.

"Night Rockers let's rock" Partho hollered.

Howrah

It was our first class test of strength of materials. We four were sitting according to our set cheating arrangement. We just had pens with us but Sid had cardboard with best of luck written on it and had half a dozen pens.

"Don't know why, I don't feel like taking the test" Yash said yawning. These don't-know-why things are very strange.

"Me too" I repeated my two favourite words. Such small words and such a deep meaning. I was too busy with Sonia and could not prepare well for the tests. Although I trusted Sid and Chain Reaction, but there was always a chance of getting caught. One should prepare individually for atleast getting pass marks, but this time I wasn't prepared at all.

"Can't the test be cancelled?" Yash said.

"It's simply impossible" Sid said.

"You shut up Idiot." Viks slammed him before he could say anything further.

"Atleast we can talk to Sir" Yash said.

"But what excuse will we give?" I asked.

"Maybe health reason" Yash said.

"But it's the silliest and dumbest of the excuse. Afterall all four of us can't give medical excuses" Viks said.

"Let's go to sir and think of a better excuse on the way" Yash said.

"But who will talk to the Prof?" I asked. Yash and Sid hid their faces.

"I know I will have to. You all don't have that courage" Viks said.

"But cancelling test is not a good thing. I want to take the test today. I had put a lot of effort and I came fully prepared today." Sid said again.

"Shut up and come with us" Viks scolded him. Sid is a kid, needs to get scolded every time. Even in engineering college he wants to study as we did in class eighth.

We went to the third floor to talk to sir. There were cabins of only two Profs on the third floor-and the other Prof was absent. Prof's cabin was open. We entered the cabin.

"Sir.....sir" I shouted. But no reply came as he was not there.

"Is he in the toilet?" Yash enquired and then went to check the toilet.

"Yes he is in the toilet." He confirmed after noticing the locked door.

"Guess what I'm going to do now?" Viks said winking his eyes.

"Lock the professor?" Yash said

"Yo" Viks said

"But what if something bad happens and we get caught" Sid said frightened.

"Mr Kid, I mean Sid. Can't you see Sir's cell is on his table and there is no one except us and Sir on this floor?"

He locked the Prof in the toilet and we ran downstairs making minimum noise. We heard the Prof knocking the door, but we were sure no one would listen to his knockings and come to help .We went to the classroom and sat there with other classmates so that no one doubts us. After fortyfive minutes when the Prof didn't come everyone started worrying. Now when it was almost sure that the test was cancelled for that day, Viks shouted "Hey! I think Prof came today. I saw him in the morning."

"I saw him too" Subojit said.

"Let's go and check if he's in his cabin." Debdeep said.

"Hey! I'm leaving. If anything happens, give me a missed call." I told Yash.

"Where are you rushing to?" Viks asked

"As if you don't know? Sonia of course" Yash said

"Enjoy buddy" Viks said.

It was Saturday a half-day. After the class test getting cancelled, I bunked the rest of three classes for going to Howrah with Sonia. This time I decided the place. I knew Howrah Bridge and ferry boats can be the most romantic sites for dating.

She came rushing, adjusted her hair, drank a sip of water from her bottle and then said "You know how I managed to come? Mom doubts too much when I go out on Saturdays and Sundays."

"But you are excellent at fooling your mom." I said with a mild smile.

We sat in the bus E-1 to go to Howrah. We shared one earphone each, while we were listening to the FM. As we got down on Howrah station someone passed a comment "Look these 10th class students are running away from their home"

I saw a smile on her face, probably because she was called student of class 10th, meaning she looked underage. Girls can sink to any level to hide their age.

"Let me deal with him" I said folding my full sleeves shirt up.

"Leave na. One should ignore these things"

Frankly speaking I never had the intention of fighting with that person. I acted a bit to show Sonia that I was not a coward.

Howrah Bridge is really an engineering miracle. Walking with her on the epitome of strength, with breezy air coming from Hooghly it felt awesome. I saw the large riveted joints and suddenly I realised that I was also a future engineer. The beauty of Howrah Bridge was breath-taking. I was walking with an engineering beauty on one side and a natural beauty, Sonia on the other. Can't judge who was better. Actually they were totally different types of beauties. One was soft but other was hard and gigantic tall. I was thinking if Sid would come with his girlfriend, if he could make any, then he would teach her about these rivets and truss and all.

We went to the ticket counter of the ferry boat.

"Where to?" The man at the counter asked.

"Give ticket for the longest route" I said.

He looked at both of us and smiled, and gave the tickets.

The ferry boat was mostly empty. It was great scenery outside; the boat knifing through the water and the water splashing all around, the cool atmosphere and a feeling of joy. I love water. Maybe Viks would not like such scenery or this place.

"Why do you love me?" She asked me in the ferry.

"What?" The ferry was making noise; so I had to put an extra effort to listen to what she was saying.

"What do you like in me? Why you love me so much? You could have got a better girl." She said.

I had doubt on the third question, but for the other two I had answers.

"I love everything in you. I love your big kajal lined eyes. I love your daily changing earrings, especially that dolphin one. I love your small 3 no. feet. I love your voice. I love your smile. I love the way you say repeatedly No No No No when you have to deny something. Your long hairs and your small lips and..."

"You're crazy. You notice so much!" She interrupted before getting my list complete.

"A true mad lover. Now you say what do you like in me?" I asked her.

"I like everything in you"

"Like what?"I asked her. I wanted the complete list, as I did for her.

"Your eyes" She said. This was strange. You generally don't expect girls to praise your eyes. It is generally our job. And when did she see my eyes. They were hidden behind specs.

"And?" I wanted her to say more. Everyone likes to be praised.

"Your smile"

"And?"

"I like the whole you" Her list ended. Only three things in the list? I was clearly unhappy and not at all satisfied. I wanted more admiration. "Now stop acting like a kid. I love you" She said, probably noticing the disappointment on my face.

"I love you too" Still half-satisfied. I began to look at the splashing water to change my mood.

"I thought of telling you a thing. We are getting too close. I know you guys want it fast but I don't want that thing early" Sonia said breaking the lull. I knew what 'that thing' she was talking about.

"Actually I support you in this. And I don't believe in physical love. We can have it when we both are ready for it. If you want we can have it after marriage, but if possible try to do it a little early." It was Mr Gentleman and a real man with some desire, both speaking at the same time. Only I know the weight of stone I put on my heart to say what I said.

After two three rounds on the ferry boat we were hungry. We went to Food Plaza, the best restaurant in that area (that I knew) and the food was good and reasonable also.

It was evening by the time we left Food Plaza.

"Let's go to the Millennium Park. It's just two minutes from here" I said.

"Parks! They are so cheap! You know what they do there and that too so openly" Sonia replied.

"We won't be doing anything like those cheap couples. We would just sit and talk" I assured her.

"You better remember your words or else I'll leave"

Sitting on a bench facing Hooghly River, the whole place felt extremely romantic with the light getting dimmer. Gentle breezes were waving her hairs which I was playing with my left hand which was around her shoulders. And in my right hand I held her hand.

"Chana garam...chana garam" A lady vendor came bawling. And she cemented her beside us like statue.

"We don't need it. Go away" Sonia said.

"Memsaab. Everyone in this park buys this. You will also have to buy. Please buy babuji." Lady said more like commanding. "Or else I'll be standing here only." She said murmuring. Oh! So this was the trick-to snatch away the privacy of love-buds. You buy it or else, there was no else, you have to buy it.

"How much for it?" I said

"10 Rupees shaab." She took the money and went bawling again "Chana garam" and taking the location advantage in the business.

"You know how much I love swimming. I wish I could swim just now. Water just pulls me. I even won school championship in swimming." She said looking at water while I was just looking at her sparkling nose pin.

"So you are Sonia Mirza of Swimming. Hey you copy Sania Miza, don't you? You have this nose pin and your name is also Sonia. Sonia copies Sania"

"Shut up, you idiot" She said.

"Hey wait wait wait! Jokes apart, if you were school champion then why didn't you try further? For higher levels?" I asked her. It was a genuine question.

"I applied but wasn't selected. Actually they rejected me on medical grounds."

"Why were you overweight then?" I said jokingly. It was difficult to imagine how this ~~41~~ forty one Kg girl could be overweight. Imagining this I was smiling.

"No dumbo. My pulse rate is abnormal"

"What? What does it mean?"

"I mean my pulse rate is abnormally high. 100 per minute is my average. It's congenital."

I didn't believe it. So I took her hand and counted her pulse myself and a strange inexplicable sensation gripped me and my heart thumped.

"What......... What is its effect?" I asked stammering.

"It decreases longevity"

Her words hit me in torment. I was shaken from inside. My smile went flying with the breeze. My ability to think and speak ceased temporarily.

She put her hand on my knees and said "Say something. Why are you quiet?"

I tried to control but the bloody gravity pulled it and a drop of tear from my eyes fell on her hand. She took her hands back to see what was it and said "Rahul! You are crying?"

When someone asks this question it makes a path for more tears to come. I completely broke into tears. I was crying like baby holding her. "No I won't let you die. I love you" I snuffled.

"Oh my baby. Cry. Cry more." What? What did she say? I thought she would tell me to stop crying but instead she told me to cry more? I moved my head to other side.

"Men should cry. It reduces chance of heart attack as they have a million unexpressed feelings inside them." she said. Wasn't it too unromantic?

"And you don't worry, doctor said it only might decrease longivity. The probablity is very less. Now put away your worries and show me your yellow teeth. C'mon smile now!" She said.

I had never cried in the past two years. I was myself surprised that I was crying for a girl. Excuse me, was this real love?

Viks was sitting in his towel as he had given all his clothes to laundry. On his long legs the small towel was looking like mini skirt. But his hairy legs were hardly sexy, atleast for us.

"Where were you the whole day?" He blocked the entrance with his legs and asked me like those cheap constables of the 70s movies.

"What happened to the Prof?" I asked changing the topic.

"Guess what? Rohit opened the toilet and bang! One slap on his face. We all escaped. Later the Prof cooled down but he wanted to know who locked him inside" Yash again

"He'd never know" Viks said with confidence.

He removed his leg barrier and allowed me to enter the room.

"Let's go to the mess. I'm feeling hungry" Viks said.

"I won't go. I'm already full" I said.

Yash was searching Viks' least dirty pajama to wear. I took my cell to call Sonia.

"Whom are you calling?" Viks asked.

"Sonia. Why?"

"Whole day you were with Sonia and now you're calling her again?" Viks said.

"Can't I talk? She is my girlfriend"

"How do you stand girls? I mean how you spend hours and hours with her without getting bored. Girls are so boring." Viks said

"When your love is true you won't ever get bored." I replied.

What do you talk over the phone with her? What 'baniyan' you wear or bra in case of girls?"

"You're crossing the limit. Don't interfere in my personal matters.

Afterall you're just a friend, not my brother or soul mate"

"Hey don't be senti Rahul" Yash was such a person who always kept things cool.

"Don't tease him Viks."

"You go and talk to Sonia. Happy?"

I pressed button 3 of my cell hard, the speed-dial for Sonia. I loved her.

Dharma Bhrashtha

I was about to enter the 10:20 am Maths Class. The Prof was already in the class as I was late by two minutes. I had to miss my meal in the mess for attending this class as I had 0 out of 8 attendances.

"May I come in sir" I asked and entered the classroom being sure that the Prof would say yes. Two minutes late is kind of okay. Asking the Prof was just a matter of formality.

I was heading towards our last bench, where we sat even if we reached the empty class. Yash and Viks had just arrived and were standing just outside the class.

"Come inside" I signalled them, still halfway to 'our' last bench.

The professor suddenly turned and said "How dare you enter the class?"

"Sir... Aaaaaaa....I asked you" I mumbled tremblingly. I was taken aback.

"Didn't you listen when I said no?" he shouted at top of his lungs.

Did he really say no? I never heard that. Viks and Yash were smiling from outside. The professor couldn't see them as they hid behind the door.

"And where is your bag."

I did not, rather could not say a word. What else could I say?

"And you don't even have a copy. And where is your pen?"

I looked down and kept quiet again. Sid carried my copy in his bag. And pen I borrowed from other classmates.

"See the boys these days. They are just heroes. They come to college without copy and pen. They just come to enjoy"

"And they come late and enter the class without permission. And that too without copy and pen"

"Sorry sir" I muttered in the lightest of my voice, more like formality than apology.

"What are you waiting for? Get out now." He said get out with the intensity to slap my ears and push me out of the class.

"Thank you" I murmured when I reached the gate. As if I cared about the class.

We went to the Ashirbad canteen after that and ordered chilly potato and paratha. Yash ordered egg curry as he was eggitarian now. Bengal is heaven for non-vegetarian people and by the same logic it is hell for pure vegetarians like me. Here we are treated as non-non-vegetarians. We get veg items with great difficulty and in most cases we are forced to join the mainstream like Yash did.

But here I have to clear confusion. Yash eats eggs but doesn't eat chicken. But what is egg? Egg is a baby chicken and would become a chicken one day, if allowed to develop. So isn't being an eggiteran is same as being non-vegeterian?

"Hey guys let's catch the morning show of James Bond. It costs just 50 rupees" Viks said.

"Great idea" Yash supported.

I kept quiet here also. Maybe it was a silent day for me. I had promised Sonia to go with her. How could I go with Viks? I thought to tell this after having food. A hungry man is harder to deal with than a full-stomached.

"Here comes the food. Have it fast. The show starts at 11:30" yash said.

We finished the food in five minutes and washed our hands in next one. Now I had to tell them.

"Hey Yash. I can't go for the movie today with you. I have promised Sonia to go with her today" I chose Yash to tell these things because he was a composed man.

"So you are not coming with us?" Viks said as he also heard me.

"Come with us na. You meet her daily. We haven't seen any movie together since two months. You will have to come." Viks said and held my hand and pulled me. I tried to resist but my strength was nothing in front of him and he lugged till some distance.

"Look Viks! Please let me go" I said.

"Are we not important for you?" Viks said.

"You are. But just think. Movie will end at 2 or 2:30 and it will be 3 as we reach here."

"Ya. You can go with her after that"

"No but we have different plans. We had planned to spend the whole day together"

"Don't be your girlfriend's pet." That was seriously annoying. I didn't reply to this.

"Look at him. How much important the girl is for him, for which he is forgetting our friendship. Remember in any case our friendship would be months older than your relationship. We became your friends first and then after one whole month she came into the picture. So our frienship is one month older." He barked again. This was heights!! Who was he to tell me all this?

"Okay let's apply your logic only. How long will you be with me? Tell me. Four years. May be a year more than that. But Sonia; She will be with me for the whole life. Now tell me." I paused to take breath.

"She is really important for me and I love her; more than anything else. So, dare not interfere in my personal matters again. Got it?" I paused again. You have to breathe more when you get agitated.

"Friends are temporary but girlfriends are forever" I said and stopped finally. Yash and Viks were both standing startled. I'm usually a composed man I rarely get angry so this was a new thing for them.

"Go go go. You go. We won't stop you." Viks said but now with a moderate voice. Perhaps he was hurt.

I went to meet Sonia straight away. One benefit of having girlfriend in college is that you can meet her everyday and college is not that bad a place for dating, especialy JU. Agreed its engineering faculty was real conservative India, but the arts faculty side was like France or something. You could see copules hanging out, walking hand in hand hugging and kissing. But in engineering faculty side we were afraid even to walk with any girl. If any prof ever saw us hanging out with girls, the practical marks showed its direct concequences.

She was sitting over the construction place from where we went to the MBA canteen.

We had our lunch together almost every day in the college canteen. We generally shared the same item in one plate because she believed eating together in the same plate enhances love. If one plate was insufficient then we had another item but again together in one plate. These modern girls and their age old superstitions! I guess Indian girls, doesn't matter how much modern they become, can't get rid of two things, superstitions and Phuchka.

The college canteen had a very limited menu and many(read all) of the items included in the menu were awful. So we were left with limited items and most of them tasted the same with different labels over them. After extensive researches on the items we found only two items suitable, fried rice,and chowmein. Previously we used to have Dosa but the day we got cockroach inside, we abandoned it. Although there were some subcategories in chowmein also but we were stuck with veg chow because I was vegetarian.

"I'm bored of having the same stuff daily. Can't we have something else? I want to eat chicken chow today" said Sonia.

"No problem. You take chicken and I'll take veg" I replied.

"But we should have in the same plate"

"Don't be so superstitious. Nothing will happen if we eat in different plates for one day"

"No way. I don't want our love to get reduced."

I had to agree to what Sonia said. She gave the logic that, the chicken chow they give here was veg chow plus chicken pieces in the side of the plate with veg chow. So I can have the veg side. Plus she told me that she'd feed me with her hands. I thought it would feel as if I was back to my childhood times and my mom was feeding. I missed this part of my life plus thinking of romantic possibilities I agreed to her.

She washed her hands and splashed water on her face in the meantime the food was to arrive.

"Do you have a hanky? I forgot mine today." She asked me and I gave mine.

"Yucks! This is yesterdays hanky na? You dirty guy! You don't even change hankies daily, so disgusting" She said holding the corner of the hanky with thumb and index finger.

Yesterday's hanky? What the shit? What was the problem in using yesterday's hanky? We used it for weeks. I never even brought hankies before I met her. I used my pocket instead for drying my hand; put your wet hand into your pocket and you take out dry!!!

"Go and wash your hand now. You dirty guy. Don't you wash your hands before eating?"

I went to wash hand. Suddenly it came to my mind that I already had food only half an hour back in the Ashirbad Canteen.

"Oh I forgot I had eaten only half an hour back. I won't eat" I said.

"Your wish" She replied.

She started eating. I opened the flap of my mobile's camera and started taking her pics.

I just love Chinese dishes and couldn't resist myself from having atleast a fork of chowmein.

I noticed her staring at my face with a hidden smile.

"Why are you looking at me like this?" I said gulping the food swiftly.

She smiled and then burst into laughter again, in her usual style.

"Now what happened mam?" I asked.

"The chow you just gulped had a small piece of chicken in it" she said grinning.

"What? Why didn't you stop me?" I said with my eyes wide open and I was feeling like throwing up.

"I'm sorry" She held my hand.

"This is really bad. Why you did this. Don't you know I'm a Brahmin? You defiled my religion. You *made my dharma brashtha.*" My rage was on its extreme. My voice begun rising exponentially.

"Do you have any respect for me and my religion? You cunning girl. I trusted you." I said in a voice loud enough to make Hitler frightened. Everyone in the canteen started looking at us.

"Hey I'm sorry. I didn't do anything. You yourself ate it."

"But you could have told me. Go to hell now" I jerked her hands off, pushed the chair and kicked the table hard. The plate fell to the ground.

"Don't create a scene now." She murmured.

"Create scene?" I banged a tight slap on her face.

I left the canteen and went to the PCB and sat there. Bad day it was, first the prof, then Viks and then Sonia -everyone left me fuming.

She followed me till the PCB and sat on the other side, 180 degrees opposite to me. She was not crying but sobbing sound was easily perceptible.

"Why are you sitting here? Go home" I taunted her

"You asked for this, so I bought this for you today. I'm going home now." She said taking out a photo album from her bag. It had her childhood and school pics.

She kept the photo album beside me and continued crying and hid her face with her hands.

God has gifted this special lifeline to babies and women-tears. Though I didn't mean to make her cry, but maybe she deserved this. She gave me chicken to eat, broke my trust. She could have stopped me. I never ate this thing. ..Or I ate just once before, but that was by mistake. It happened when I asked for Veg fried rice in CET Canteen. The canteen boy gave some gravy on it. One day I asked for Veg items available there and they showed me only three items and when I asked about the 'tasty' gravy they gave me, I was traumatized. It was the gravy of chicken chilly. I bathed with Ganga-water which my nani gave in a bottle. I forgot this deliberately, until this day which reminded me of it. So this was not my first encounter with chicken.

So why was I angry with Sonia . I could easily see the imprint of my hand on her white face in the shades of red. How to handle the situation now? What to do next? I started conversation by saying, "Hey! Sonia. I'm sorry. I just got..."

"Don't talk to me. I know it's entirely my fault" she interrupted in between. When girls accept all their faults they are really in a sad sulking mood. I knew things wouldn't be cooling down so easily and I was ready for it. After 15-20 consecutive attempts of saying her sorry, my patience began to surrender and I knew something extraordinary had to be done. Suddenly my eyes fell on my hand and then my little finger and then the ring I was wearing. My little finger's size meant roughly Sonia's ring finger. A great idea circulated into my mind. I took the ring off my finger and whispered into her ears "Look A.B. is behind you" A.B. was a Prof of her department and she had a crush over him, actually many of her friends had. Don't know how these girls can adore this forty-nine year Prof who probably can't do anything with them(because he was married). Frankly speaking I felt jealous of him.

I knew she would surely turn back to see her crush and she did. I was quick enough in doing my job. I inserted the ring in her ring finger.

"Here goes our ring ceremony. We're engaged now" I said smiling.

It took her a moment to realise what had happened. She glared me then the ring, gave a smile and broke into another cry. But I guess, these were the tears of happiness. Girls have to cry over everything happy or sad.

"Please don't cry" I said and her rate of flow of tears increased. Never say this to any girl coz it only makes them cry more.

"Please stop now. I've no experience of consoling crying girls" I said.

"Know one thing? If my nani ever comes to know about this, she'll kill me and your plan of becoming her grand-daughter in law will be doomed." I said with an innocent face. She smiled, I felt relieved.

"You are smiling at my demise. What if the chicken I just ate lays an egg in my stomach?" The worst PJs make girls laugh the most.

"Chicken doesn't lay eggs. Hens do." She said and continued laughing nonstop and her cheeks again turned tomato red. She was looking gorgeous. We remembered this day with its special name – 'dharma bhrastha'

I opened the album and saw all the pics and selected five. Three of the pics were her school pic. She looked so pretty in school dress. The rest two pics were of her aunt's marriage where she was wearing saree. She had also put some light makeup and was looking awesome. Indian girls look best in saree.

"I'm taking these five pics"

"No no. Don't take it. What will I say in home if my mom asks?"

"She won't ask. No one remembers how many photos they put in an album."

"Okay keep them." She said.

"I love you" I said. Girls repeatedly want to listen this as if they always forget and need to be reminded again and again.

"I love you too"

Sanskriti

It was March-the time of Sanskriti -the cult fest of JU. Our band was to participate in the competition. Though NIGHT ROCKERS was not among the biggy bands but atleast we got into one. Though Yash was the lead guitarist, I got in as the extra singer or better called chorus.

We didn't get much time to practice, two weeks were not sufficient. And the D-day arrived sooner than we anticipated.

The name of our band was announced and we got up the stage. We had decided to perform two songs – Aadat by Jal band and Smoke On the Water in the allotted ten minutes.

We started with the raga of Aadat sung by Raghu, the lead singer and Yash played its tabs while drummer Rajeev was beating his drums and Partho was on the keyboard.

Right from the beginning, I sensed we were missing something. We were playing just for the sake of playing; there was no feel and enthu. Plus our co-ordination was not that good. And when music doesn't come from heart, it can't be good.

"Ab to aadat si hai aise jeene me.." we were ending the first song.

And it didn't take audience too long before they started hooting and booing "You suck."

"Get down" Someone shouted. I closed my eyes as I was close to tears. It is never easy to stand in front of 1000 booing audience. As soon as our first song ended we were told to get down the stage by the judges. We weren't even allowed to perform the second song.

It was a really awful performance, rather pathetic. I had never been more humiliated in my life.

Euphoria was the guest band on that full moon night. I was sitting at the back of the Open Air Theartre(OAT) with Sonia. Yash, Sid and Viks were dancing in the front with the entire crowd.

"Let's leave now. It will be quite a rush at the end of the show" I said to Sonia, half an hour before the end of the show.

"No I want to hear mayeri. It's my favourite." She said. Euphoria saved the best songs for the last.

Meanwhile I saw Yash and Viks lifted Sid and threw him in air and then caught him back as he descended. They were having their fun and I was having mine. Sitting hand in hand on a full moon night with your girlfriend and Euphoria performing live in front is like a heaven created for you.

Meanwhile her mom called her and she was worried about how Sonia would come back alone so late. And when Sonia told her that I would leave her till home, she was relaxed. My to-be mom-in-law trusted me even when she still thought us as just friends (and not lovers).

The show got over at 9:45. The exit was more than overcrowded. Thousands of students, all wanted to leave the OAT just then. I wrapped her into my arms to save her from the crowd and rush. I had to do this because all the drunken guys were rushing and pushing everyone. And we didn't have time to wait as we were already too late.

"Oh shit! My sandal has broken" I said when I saw my sandal after we came out surviving. She bent a little to see my broken sandal. "Girlfriends are big responsibilities. If I were single I would have slept cosy in my bed by this time" I said.

"You should have thought before" She said grinning. By the time we reached her house it was half past ten; late enough to make her mom come outside her home and watch the way for her daughter.

"You got so late. You never think how much worried I get when you come late" MIL(Mom In Law) said.

"Mom it was great show tonight. And Rahul was with me, so you didn't have to worry"

"How would I not worry, you are my only asset. Now come in fast. I've prepared food for both of you"

"No aunty I have to go. It's already quite late" I said.

"No beta. Have the food and then go"

"Come Na" Sonia said.

"It's late. You must be hungry too. It won't take too long. And where will you eat, the college mess would get closed by the time you'd reach there" MIL argued. She had a point.

"No excuses. You're coming" Sonia said tugging my shirt.

I reached her flat on the fourth floor by stairs, as there was no lift-trademark of economical flats. There were two bedrooms, both not too big, but decorated with all sorts of curtains and table-cloth and wind-chimes and wallpapers and all. Everything was looking very girly as if no male had entered the house for a long time, which I guess was correct. And suddenly it came, which I guess was the only male who lived with them-Max, their dog. It came and started sniffing me and licking me and I hate when any dog does that. I hate dogs.

"Don't be afraid. He won't do anything" Sonia said.

"Let him sniff you for a moment, let him recognise you and then he'd not do anything. Sonia take Rahul to your room, I'm getting food quickly." MIL said.

"I'm a little afraid of dogs" I said wiping off drops of sweat which I either had due to climbing stairs or because of Max.

"Don't call him dog. Call him Max. He's my son." She said as we entered her room.

"Son? So you're unmarried mother huh?"

"Shut Up you idiot. By the way have you ever thought about our life after marriage? How many kids do you want?" she asked which I guessed was a response to the word 'unmarried mother'.

"I want two" I said "one boy and one girl"

"What will be their names?"

Girls love these things -Planning mundane things in life. I didn't even reach the marital age yet and she was planning for our kids, definitely longer than five year plan.

We searched various websites on her PC for Kids' names and finalised four, two boys' and two girls' names so that in whatever combination we had kids we could have their names pre-decided.

The names were Rajat, Rimi, Sonali and Shanu. We had plans that of the two kids, one would have name starting with R and other with S.

Aunty got the food and we turned the screen of the PC off. The food was really tasty. I wanted to eat plates and spoon also but had to control myself in my In-Laws'-House. Thank God, all aunties in Kolkata don't cook badly. I took my hanky out after I washed my hand after the dinner. Yes, this time I had a clean hanky.

"The food was excellent aunty." I said.

"Thanks. You better leave now. Or you won't get any conveyance. And ya do come again here."

Ya aunty, I'll have to come here again and again, I wanted to say.

We were getting down the stairs. Sonia came to see me off.

"Weather is good na?" Sonia said.

I knew this was her signal. It meant her mood was really good and if I kiss her she won't say no. Being so close to a girl you come to know about these subtle signals.

But I was in her house; I didn't have the courage to do these things at her place. I mean what if her mom saw us. Or what if anyone else in the apartment saw us and complained to her mother plus gossip among themselves, combo damage. I dropped the plan.

"Rahul, don't go"

"Why?"

"Because" She said and kissed me. Girls do these things so gently, so elegantly, so gracefully, unlike us guys who just act like dogs with our tongues out, showing our despo attitude. Girls are like cats and guys are like dogs. Guys can start anywhere but girls, they are very wary. And you see that's why girls' walk is called cat-walk. Close observance of the two would show the immense resemblance.

“Come. Let’s go in the backyard of my house. I know a place there” She said.

“Are you mad? This is your house. If we get caught you know what can happen”

But when girls are in mood they hardly listen.

“This is my house. I know it better than you. Come fast” She said pulling my sleeves.

We went to the backyard of her house. I told her to open her hair. And I was playing with her soft, smooth and silky hair. A very beautiful fragrance was coming out of her hair. And how beautiful girls look with their hairs are open. I wished the hair band wasn’t invented at all.

“You know what? I introduced you to my mom today, one day I’ll tell her about our relation and then about marriage. I’m so happy today”

I kissed her again. She was looking so gentle. The air was cold and wind began to flow and her hair started waving. She was looking all the more beautiful.

“Will your mom support our relation?”

“She definitely will, I know her. She is the best mom in the world. After he left, I don’t want to take his name; my mom was both Dad and Mom for me. She loves me so much and so do I”

When were about to kiss again her cell begun to ring. She always carried her cell with her fearing that her mom would see our SMSes.

“Oh my God! Mom is calling. I’m going bye” She started running.

“My last kiss?” I shouted.

She came kissed me and said “Love you” and she ran upstairs after that.

I went to the main road from where I could get a conveyance.

I always withdrew Rs 100 from my ATM on a daily basis. With today's hundred rupee spent, I was almost empty with just 7-8 rupees in my pocket. Though they were sufficient for auto fare but at 12 where would one find an auto in Kolkata? And I couldn't afford a taxi so I walked with my broken sandal limping and dragging. Dogs often barked and chased me. And the patrolling police gave me a look as if I was a terrorist.

In between my walk to the hostel I got 2 SMSes from her.

"My mom ws tellin abt tht u r gud bt u r 2 short. Bt overall u r nice n decent."

"She told Max "see ur dad" showing ur pic. I thnk she's doubtng"

The Break

Semester ended. The summer break began. I was leaving for my hometown. I was sitting with Sonia but she was maintaining a pin drop silence since the last 10 minute.

"Say something. I'm leaving today. Don't you want to talk to me?"

"Can't you stay for few more days?" Finally she said something sobbing. I lifted her face and her eyes were red and had tears in them.

"I'm not going on a battle-field that you are crying. I'm going just for two months dear."

"Just?"

We were being separated for the first time for so long since our relation started. We exchanged many 'I love you" and 'will miss you'. Sonia promised to chat with me every day on Yahoo Messenger. We made our resolutions to call each other atleast once a day. After that, I left for hostel for packing my luggage and Sonia left for RKM. I stuffed the clothes inside the suitcase in 10 minutes and took E-1 bus.

"Where are you? Have you reached Howrah? You haven't even left Kolkata and I've started missing you. Don't know how I will live these 60 days?" her SMS came when I was in bus.

I called her the very next moment "I'm in bus. Where are you?"

"I'm getting out of RKM." She replied.

"What the...My bus is standing here only at the traffic signal near RKM. Hey I can see you" I said taking my head out of the window. The fellow passengers thought that I went mad.

I got down and ran to her. "God is great. He wanted us to meet once more. But you had your RKM class na?"

"It got cancelled"

"Hey Sonia! I want something as your memory which I'd always see and remember in these two months"

"What can I give? I don't have anything to give"

"Think fast. I don't have time. Signal can open any moment. Hey how about your ear-rings?"

She made no objections and started opening her dolphin ear-rings.

"You know how much I love your dolphin ear-rings and you"

"Now don't make me cry more. Go into your bus. The signal is yellow" She said handing the ear-rings to me. I saw the eyes. They were wet again.

"I love you" I said kissing the ear-rings and came back into bus.

This wasn't the first of the coincidences. There were many more amusing coincidences. Whenever I SMSed her, I got her another SMS from her before I got the delivery report of my SMS, as if our timing was synchronised. And this was not all. Whenever I called her I always found her number busy, and would later come to know that she was also trying my number at the very moment.

Even if the weighing machine refused to accept this fact, this time also Nani said "You are getting thin day by day. Don't they give you food or what?"

Sonia and I chatted and called daily as per the promise. I called her with the money saved from phuchka and samosa allowance. And rest money which I got by buying only 900 grams of vegetable when nani told to buy 1 Kg. This was because while I was in home I never got any pocket money. I was still like a school child for Nani who thought poket-money would spoil me.

DAY 10

We were chatting on Yahoo Messenger while playing Doodle. We played tic-tac-toe first. Then we had a painting competition between us, which Sonia won. Then we made our wedding card.

I: How much do you love me?

Sonia: More than my life

I: God forbid, but if ever we ever break up then what would you do?

Sonia: I'll die. I simply can't live without you

I: I'll die without you too. I can't live without you

Sonia: You copy-cat. You always have to copy whatever i say.

I: I'm not copying but we are naturally so similar. We never had a fight like other couples do?

Sonia: Touch wood. Till now we never had. But I want to see how it feels. Wana fight?

Rahul: Ya sure. We should have a pseudo fight. We'll have one when I come back.

Sonia: Sure. Now tell me, I'm bengali and you are not. By which tradition would we marry? Bengali way or your way?

Rahul: We'll do by both rituals. But you know I like Christian marriages the most. And so I'll marry in Christian way also.

Sonia: How many times will you marry me?

Rahul: the maximum number of times I can do. I want to be with you for the rest of my incarnations.

Sonia: Know one thing. I like Thailand's marriage also

Rahul: We'll do that also. All experiments with my one and only wife.

DAY 35

You can't be agreeing over anything and everything. Fights and clashes are essential part of love life. I and Sonia too were having regular fights since past one week. The reasons were strange, very weird indeed. And there were no solutions to the problems as they were as a result of our basic differences, our cultures, the way we were brought up. Since the last 20 calls either of us hung up the call in between. Then there were rounds of sorry saying and we won't fight again, but of no use. The stupid fights were starting to get serious. Actually when things like this start, you tend to doubt and hate everything about each other. You can't overlook even the smallest of the differences. I never knew we had so many differences. And we had to adjust.

We were chatting today after three days. We promised not to fight today and have normal talks. I thought of talking romantically today and tried to forget the past few days.

I: I don't want to fight dear. I'm tired of these daily fights.

Sonia: Neither do I want to fight. But you say something and ignite my anger.

I: As if you don't do anything?

Sonia: Don't start again. You remember promise?

I: Ya. Let's talk of something else. Let's talk of marriage. Our marriage.

Sonia: Do you realise dear you haven't reached marriageable age yet, I don't have a problem otherwise ;)

She always used too much of smileys

I: But I want to get married early, say at 25. I want you to love me like anything, which I never got.

Sonia: I love you and I'm with you. But I don't want to marry early. You'd be an engineer at 22, but it takes time in general line.

I: Why are you worrying so much? I am there to earn the bucks for you. I promise that I'd earn more than you can spend.

Sonia: I don't want to get dependent on your money. I want to be independent. I want my position in society. You may have this tradition at your place but sorry, I can't just sit and cook for you and wait for you to return from office. I can't stay all alone in house and get bored.

I: I don't have problem with your job or your studies, but you can do your studies after marriage. I'd support you in that.

Sonia: Don't teach me okay. I know studying after marriage is just not possible. I knew there are many responsibilities. I want a good life.

I was getting irritated.

I: What job can you get with your socio degree? A teacher? That's it. Don't fly too much.

Sonia: Mind your language. Don't treat me as if I'm inferior. I'm doing my animation course diploma plus I'm learning German and I also have interest in film making which I have as my side subject. I have many options open.

I: Sorry for what I said. But you should think about me. I want a family which I can call my own, I need love.

Sonia: I also ask the same from you. You should also think about me. And anyways I'm always with you, so how does marrying matters?

I: You argue too much. That's what I don't like in you. Whatever you say, I want you to look after my child very well.

Sonia: What does that mean?

I: I mean my kid shouldn't feel neglected as I did in my childhood times. I don't want that they have to cater the food for themselves when they return from school. I don't want my kids to feel the same way. Atleast one parent should be home when he or she returns from home.

Sonia: Why don't you say directly what you mean?

I: I want you to quit job after we have a kid.

Sonia: So you want me to sacrifice everything? My job, everything? This is what a good Indian woman should do? Sorry I'm not like that. All I can ensure you that I'll take good care of them.

I: If you want, you can do part time job, but in no way I want my kids to feel neglected

Sonia: Part time? You always underestimate me. At this moment I feel that we shouldn't plan kids. Let's just don't have kids? Will that be fine?

I: Know one thing? Only pros don't want kids and don't look after them.

I don't know what I said, why I said, what it meant. I just know what happened next – she went offline. I didn't mean this. I didn't intend to hurt her. I don't know why I used the word pros? I just wanted her to agree with me. It always happens with us guys that we want to say something but end up saying something else. And we even don't know the probable consequences.

DAY 36

Her message came in morning. "You're a 15th century man n I can't continue with you. It's better we part off. I respect your point of view, but I tell u frankly, I got this feeling of late that I'm not the girl 4 u. You better find a girl who can do this much for you, and keep you happy forever."

And then her call came. I picked up and said "I'm sorry. I know you're angry with me coz of what I said last day"

"No. I'm not angry with you. Don't think it is a hurried decision, I was thinking about it right from the day I felt we were different. Very different."

"But we were having so many similarities"

"Ya we had similarities but you see, we are very different on the ground level. Even if we continue now, the chance is very less that we will make a happy couple. I talked to many friends about this and they agreed with what I'm saying to you now"

"Please don't do like this. Actually I didn't mean what I said. I mean..."

"I fully understand what you mean" She cut the phone. I saw the screen "01:01" Again 1 second.

I seriously didn't mean this. I know I was very harsh to her and hoped her to do the impossible. But I had realised now that I didn't want anything. I didn't want to marry early. And if Sonia said she would take care of my kid, she would definitely do that very nicely. I know she is very responsible. She is so good. That's why I love her so much. I was ready to take my words back. I was ready to change myself and make adjustments. I didn't want this to happen between us. She called after one minute

"So I just called to say, please don't call me again" She said.

"Please don't do like this. I'm sorry. Can't we be friends atleast?"

"I don't think it can ever happen. Friendship after relationship is very difficult. But I'll give it a thought. Bye" She said and hanged.

This unequal distribution of power is unfair. In a relation, girl is the one who accepts the proposal, and they are the one who can part off.

DAY 40

I called and SMSed her many a times, but got only one reply.

"Don't call me again and again and piss me off" She SMSed after she didn't pick the phone.

DAY 50

What could I do now? She was not picking up my calls. In no case I could go back to Kolkata before 15 days. And even when I go, will she meet me? I thought of using my first lifeline – Phone A Friend. By this time, I had acquaintance with most of her friends. I send friend requests to all of them on Orkut, some were already added in my friends list. This would give me some backing.

I had mobile nos. of a few friends in which I called up Monika.

"I've nothing to do in this" She said.

"Hey Monika. You know, we were so happy together. Can't you help me when our relation is in trouble. Your help can save our relation. Please take my side, I mean don't go against me. Please help me out. I know Sonia is angry with me"

I rephrased my words into one or other with the same meaning for the next one hour. I hung the phone after saying

"Please don't tell Sonia that I called you. She might get all the more angry"

How foolish was I to use the expression 'do not say' to girls. How could I ever think that she won't tell that to Sonia?

"How dare you disturb my friends? You are so cheap Rahul. I never expected this from you. You are asking them to support you. Asking for votes? Are you a politician or Indian Idol or what?" Her SMS came after one hour.

Things were getting worse and worse. Whatever I was doing was making thing worse as if I had anti-Midas touch. We were getting so far in so little time. I don't know what did Sonia tell her friends but all the friend requests I had sent were rejected and a few had even ignored (blocked) me.

Day 60

I returned to Kolkata, before-time as usual. I knew she would not meet me easily. But I knew she would be coming today to celebrate Monika's birthday in campus, which I came to know by her scraps. I decided to hit it there. In the enjoyment of birthday, maybe Sonia would cool down and talk to me properly. One talk was all I needed.

Just one talk, to tell her that I love her very much, to tell her that I realised my mistakes, to tell sorry for I hurt her, for everything. I knew one hour talk would solve all our problems.

I was somewhat excited and badly nervous. I was going to see and talk to her after such a long time which was like lifetimes for me. I was biting my nails which ended up soon. I wished that I had more nails to bite.

Sonia and her group came there at two, while I was waiting since twelve. I hid myself in a class-room and watched where they were supposed to sit and cut the cakes and all. They sat at the construction place. They had cakes and all the picnic material with them. There were 4 four girls and two boys, the boyfriends of two of them. While I was the missing one, the boy-friend of Sonia, the fourth girl had recently breakuped. All the girls of this group have had atleast two breakups.

One thing I would like to mention here that Debojit was Monika's third boyfriend in last one year. And Piya recently had her second break-up and was going around with Sourav. I know these girls were bitches and I used to call them break-up bitches. Don't know how Sonia clogged in this group, the only exception.

"Hi Everybody. Happy birthday Monika" I said as I approached their group while they had already cut the cakes and started partying. Everyone was glaring me with surprise and whatever. Sonia made a face which showed disgust.

"Hey birthday girl won't you offer me a piece of cake?" I asked Monika jokingly mainly to cut the tension.

There was an abominable lull. Sonia started looking away. Her face stressed, as if saying "Why did he come?"

"Don't act like you don't know anything. Don't act as if nothing has happened" Monika said.

Okay, they all were well aware of this and I was sure they would be supporting our breakup. Afterall they would want Sonia to become a break-up bitch and she would have to fulfil the criterion of having two breakups. It was no point in talking to them.

I headed towards Sonia and said "Hey Sonia, I'm sorry for whatever happened. I knew we had huge issues. But now when I've come here, I'm sure we'll be settling it down"

"But I don't want. Everything has settled after we broke-up"

"But this is not fair. Is it justified; I mean I should get a chance to tell my point."

"Was it fair when I cried for nights and nights? I'm telling we're better off without each other"

"But please talk once"

"What will she talk to you? She has nothing to talk to you. You bloody even slapped her one day. You have no right to do this to anyone. Poor girl didn't say anything to you that day" Piya said. When did I slap her? Oh! Dharma Bhrashta day. But it was Sonia's fault also. And it went in the heat of the moment. So even my one slap came into account. Who said girls are weak at calculations and keeping accounts?

I wanted to say something but was interrupted by Monika "If you ever loved her then you'd do whatever she wants. If she wants not to talk to you, you won't talk to her"

Okay these breakup bitches were giving me lessons of love???

"What? You mean a guy with one year relation has no right to console his girlfriend after a fight?" I protested.

"Don't you have anything called self respect? If you had it you'd never talk to her"

Now from where did self-respect come from? I think self-respect and love fall under two separate categories. I know they all were trying different methods to defeat me, but I won't give up. I'll get her back, I promised to myself.

"He has ruined our party. Let's go from here." Piya said.

"Hey please.." I shouted. They didn't care and left the place. Sonia was in the middle surrounded by her bodyguards who were saving her from a terrorist called Rahul.

Here she was going. My love, my everything. This was the place, construction where she was crying for me when I was going home. And now the tears were in my eyes. Life is too ironical, you see and it has bizarre co-incidences.

Alas! All in vain. I guess nothing can last forever especially happiness. This break finally led to my break-up.

Back to Operation Dog

You know what happened next. I tried operation dog. I bought a dog, took it inside metro, gifted at her, but it all flopped. A week passed since this episode. It was final match of football arena, our dept Vs Construction. Usually I don't watch football matches but I didn't have any work that day so I was in the crowd. Our team was leading 3-1 in which Viks contributed two goals. He was now a well known champ and many people envied him.

About ten minutes were left in the match. Our team just had to pass those minutes by passing and I guess we were very good at passing time. I was happy about both the match getting over and our team winning the match. I was yawning, when I saw a stone flying. And it landed on Viks. His forehead got bruised and started bleeding. He held his head and sat on the ground.

It didn't take too long for the spectators of our dept who were surrounding the field, to locate who was the culprit. They all ran like dust in the wind. I'm generally a non-violent creature but I don't know how I felt a turbulent flow of blood inside my blood vessels.

"Wait you bastard" I shouted.

By the time I reached near the culprit, the crowd surrounded and was beating him like anything. I came to know was some Shiba of Construction. Someone hit on his legs; he slipped and fell on the ground. The rest of the players came and stamped him with their spiked shoes. Rest all were hitting him with whatever they got in hand, or with their hands only. I also blessed him with three kicks and eight punches.

Viks now came with his bleeding head. He wanted to give his shot. Everyone got side when he came as happens at the time of entry of heroes in south-Indian movies. Shiba got an opportunity there and was quick enough to get up and run.

Three-four people started chasing him including me. He was running very fast, afterall he had to save himself from his hunters. The rest three gave up in the midway. But you know, I was a seventh class racing champion and how would I let my pride of consolation prize down. I chased him till the end. As I just reached him, I gave a strong push and he fell on the ground. Right from the day of my break up I felt a sudden change in my behavior, I was aggressive and abrasive.

"You bastard. You rascal what do you think. You can hit anybody and run?"

I never knew I was so powerful. I saw my power on his seventy degree turned face when I slapped him. Then I punched into his stomach and kicked on his chest. Then I banged on his nose hard which started bleeding.

Okay, it was enough damage to his body. I held his collar and pulled to lift him. But his collar came out in my hands. Then I took his sleeves and tore it, then the pocket and then left his whole shirt into rags. I never knew tearing clothes would be so easy.

"Get out of the gate and dare not enter again" I shouted at the shirtless Shiba.

"This is my college also" Shiba said.

"You get lost, or else..." This was the loudest shout of my life and it threw Shiba out of the gate no 3.

I don't know from where did I get all the aggression from? Was it because he hit Viks? Or was it the break-up?

I think they are the positive effects of break-up. They bring out your hidden aggression, which is necessary to fight with this damn world. Revenge feels good. Doesn't it?

We came back after the first aid treatment of Viks. The doctor told him to get various tests done and tied bandage round his head like turban. He was looking like sardar and was behaving like one too.

"You all supported me so well. I love you all" He said and held me tight in his arms. I held my breath.

"I'm sorry for what I said that day" I said.

"Which day?" He asked

"The day I said that friends are temporary and girls are permanent" I said looking down on ground.

"Bencho Sale. Friends never mind this much. Don't worry so much. I have forgotten these things a long time back. But wait, did I hear correctly that you two have broken up" In our case gaalis act as great adhesives. It brings a different sort of togetherness between us.

"Ya it's true. But I didn't break up. She broke up"

"How does it matter? Anyways tell me how it happened? You both were having such a good relationship"

"Leave it. Let's not spoil mood today"

"Okay so let's celebrate today in the name of long lived friendship. Free drinks by me today" Viks said.

"You know I don't drink" I said. I never drank or smoked. Viks and Yash too drunk once in a blue moon.

This is how one tries his first drink. Generally it is offered by some friend for free and there is some special occasion. I would have never drunk otherwise, but I had the pain of break-up inside me. I heard drinking gave relief Don't we all boys have a Devdas inside them?

Sid suddenly appeared like a jinnee. He came to take his copy back from Yash. He saw Yash listening to Fm with earphones plugged into his ears.

"Which song are you listening? I also want to listen. Connect it to the speakers" Sid said.

Yash took out earphones and connected its jack to the speakers. It was power 107.8 Fm which was playing "Pal Pal" from Lage raho munna bhai.

"It's so suffocating inside your room. You all are drinking? It's injurious to health" sid said

"Don't worry. I have Frooti for you." Viks said.

"Wow" Sid said. He smiled.

"The next drink in the name of friendship. Cheers !" Viks said and poured into my disposable glass.

I could not drink more. I was already full. And I did not like the taste and smell of the drink. I took another sip and felt like throwing the whole glass full of drinks into dustbin, but there you see my Brahmanism taught me not to waste the food in our plate. You see good morals always trouble you.

"Hey you all remember this song?" Sid shouted excitedly.

"Which song?" Yash asked.

Sid went to the speaker box and increased the volume and said "This song. Remember this song? This was Sonia's song. I mean the song which rang when Sonia called on Rahul's cell"

Yes it was the song "tere bin" and I set it as ringtone for Sonia. I felt despondent.

He increased the volume to maximum and said "I heard she has left you"

Isn't it a torture to make you listen the song which reminded you badly of your loved ones. And that too specifically pointing it. And that too in a tone "I heard she has left you". I wished I could hit Sid like I hit Shiba. I started looking the other side and bit my lips to control my tears.

"I think your frooti is over and you have to study also. You go. It's late now. You must return your home now." Yash said sensing my feeling.

"Oh yes. I have to study bye"

"So hero. You beat him like Sunny Deol today" Viks said to change the mood. I smiled with gratification and conceit.

"But you shouldn't have beaten him so much and that too all alone" Yash said

"Why? He did wrong and I gave him the right dose. You all also beat him. So what's the big deal" I replied.

"Ya we were in a group, so he would not be able to recognise any single person among us. But you were all alone when you were beating him. So it's sure your face must be recorded in his mind. Now what if he points you and comes with four or five people to hit you?" Yash said.

He had a point. A fluid of fear flew into my spinal cord. I never thought of this possibility when I was hitting him. "I will manage. I can manage" I told to myself.

Even after the operation dog debacle, I hadn't given up yet. And how could I? I loved her so much.

I missed her everywhere right from PCB to construction, in every corner of JU. I missed her in Inox forum, in city centre, in every mall of Kolkata. I missed her in metro rail. I missed her on the terrace where I used to sit and talk to her. I missed her at the places where I sat and thought about her. I missed her when I saw my cell and her wallpaper on it. I missed her most when I woke up from my sleep and checked my cell for her SMS. I missed her everywhere.

But my importance for her was just like a street dog. Even worse, she loved dogs.

I was sitting on the terrace at one corner and was thinking about her. I don't like crying in front of anybody. I prefer keeping my sorrows to myself. At this moment of time, my videographic memory was playing the tape of the things I lost in my life, because I didn't try hard enough or not at the correct time. My three biggest defeats I reckon were height, IIT and my parents.

I stood at the end of the assembly line in class 6, where we stood according to our height. Then my position started shifting from back to the front. I ignored it. When I was in 12 I was third in the line from the front. I always wanted to be tall but since I was 18 then, I couldn't do anything. Even when I tried my level best to increase my height by taking heightex capsule and hanging, it was too late.

The same happened with IIT-JEE exam. I was among the topper of my class. I always held a good rank in the tuitions and coaching. But as the exam was knocking the door, I lost my confidence and again ended up in failure. And I later came to know what a big mistake I had committed. I deserved IIT, but missed the tag of IITian. And I later came to know how much different is being a non-IITian from IITian in terms of reputation, facilities and campus life.

And the most painful till date, the day when my parents left each other and me. I still feel I could have done have done something, if I had worked a just little extra hard. I remember the day dad left us. He came back from office and asked mom to give a glass of water and my mom refused. And then there was a huge fight and dad left home. I still feel, maybe if I had given my dad a glass of water that day situations wouldn't be this worse.

And in the same way I was losing her-forever. Forever is very big time-for ever, the time that we can't even imagine. I won't be talking to her anymore, till the end of my life. I was really afraid thinking about this.

Are some mistakes that big that they can't be forgiven? What if one says sorry? What if one gifts a dog? What if one gives his life?

When will she forgive me? After my death? I really love her.

DMCH

I was waiting eagerly for this day to come. It was one of the many mornings after sleepless nights which I was regularly having since the last one month. Even when Sonia clearly said that, this would be the last time we were meeting, I had hopes of everything getting back to normal again. I was hoping that after today's talk, I'd make Sonia understand everything. Die-hard optimist I was. "8:30" I saw in my cellphone clock. This was the usual time she used to get up. In a steady relation you got to know every minute details of your partner's daily routine. I called her, but she didn't pick the phone up. I tried twice and thrice but there was no response from the other side. Finally I SMSed her

"Whn n whr r we meetin? Sardar-My wife is afraid of watr.Frnd-Hw did u knw? Sardar-2day I saw my wife bathing with the SecurityGuard" I always added a joke, if my message was short to complete the maximum allowed 160 characters of SMS.

Her reply came this time."Don't send me such sick messages and don't call. I'll msg u whn I get free" Okay! The messages which were very funny once were now sick. Was it the SMS or she who was sick?

"I'm free now. You can come the entrance of UG arts building" She SMSed at 11:30 when I was sitting over the PCB. Sitting alone at the places where you used to sit with your beloved can be torturous but I was getting myself in a mode so that I could talk to her most effectively.

And see these girls are limiting reagent and we guys are always excess reagent (although we are engineering guys and so had much busier schedule than those all-time-free arts girls).

I rushed to the UG Arts building to meet her. She was sitting with Piya and Monika and other girls on the stairs at the entrance of UG Arts building. They were gossiping something which was about me, I guessed. As I reached there, the girls signalled my arrival through eyes and brows. Girls have this special language of eyes. They generate waves at unique frequencies which guys can't catch. Sonia looked at me for the briefest of the time, even less than the time of exposure of film in a camera. I remembered how we met in photography club. I smiled but she was as serious as colonel 3 knot 3.

"Let's go somewhere else and talk." I said. I thought of taking her to PCB and reminding her old things. May be it would work.

"I'm not going anywhere. Whatever you've to say, say it here and make it fast" She said and the other girls talked through eyes. They wanted me to say everything in front of everyone. It was like a Court in which I was convict and girls were judges. Sonia was looking totally uninterested too. As if she just allowed me to fulfil my last desire of saying last words to her. Everything was pre-planned. The girls had already decided my fate.

"Hey! Whatever happened is not as you are thinking. It's a bit of misunderstanding. It can be sorted out if we try."

"There is no misunderstanding. Okay? And there is nothing to be sorted out."

"Hey. Give me a chance to prove myself."

"Listen Rahul Sharma, it's enough." When your girl calls you by your full name, you know it's over. "I have been crying for the past two months. And I don't want to continue this for my whole life." Okay only she was crying and I was watching Laughter Challenge.

"I couldn't sleep for nights. My whole life was disturbed. Even my studies got affected" She continued. I wanted to say that I was having very nice time and excellent sleep.

"Hey. I've changed in these months. The problems can be sorted out if we try coz I've sorted all the problems from my side."

"Don't you understand Basic English or what? There is no way can be together. Got it?" I saw a small smile on the face of other girls.

"Please just listen to whatever I'm saying"

"What will you say? Same come-back-me or I'm changed blah blah blah. No need to say anything."

"Just listen it once."

"Which part of the word NO you don't understand?"

"Hey please don't do like this. I'll die without you" I said. One friend of mine suggested me this dialogue. He got patched-up after saying this dialogue.

"No one dies. Ok? Life goes on. " She said

"No one, but me." I said and left the place. There was no use of talking to the pre-programmed girl.

I sat over the PCB again, with water in my eyes. Well, it was water only, if she doesn't reckons it. Where the hell went her every promise

"I love you more than my life." "I'll die without you"

Forget dying, she wanted to get rid of me. Can't anyone die in love? And the worst thing was I also made up these promises with her. I didn't want to be a promise-breaker like her. Was it the time to prove it? I messaged her "Don't worry I won't be troubling you anymore. I can't live without you and when you're not with. I won't live"

I waited for two minutes but reply didn't come. I closed my eyes and swallowed the whole bottle of poison I just brought from a nearby shop outside the campus. I gulped it in one go as we drink cold-drinks. I knew the amount which I took was unsafe, rather safe for getting me into trouble.

It tasted bad, my throat got chocked the very next moment. I came to the construction place for seeing her for the last time.

"Where is Sonia?" I asked Rina, her classmate. With my chocked throat, it was feeling almost impossible to speak. My eyes started watering by this time and by body sweating. She pointed at Sonia's direction.

I went and stood near Sonia. She was still with Piya and other breakup bitches.

"Sonia. Listen Sonia" I said. She was acting as if I were Mr India and she couldn't see me.

"Sonia" I said with my chocked voice. She again left me unnoticed and started walking with her group. I still was following her.

"If she doesn't want to talk to you why are you doing like this?" Piya said. But I didn't stop.

"Why don't you leave us alone in peace?" Ritika said.

They were like those NGO workers who were fighting for emancipation of women.

"Stay away. Why are you creating a scene? " Piya said.

How could I prove to them that this wasn't a scene? But enough of humiliation now!!! I left the place and walked towards the tap near Central Library. I was feeling very thirsty. I almost lost my consciousness and was trembling as I walked. It started showing its effect.

This was not as we saw in movies where everyone comes to rescue you when you're ill. I thought the girls would melt and above all Sonia would forgive me and love me for the last few hours of my life.

I was almost tumbling as I reached. I drank atleast half a litre of water but couldn't feel it because the organic matter got deposited on the inner walls of my throat. And the very next moment the water I took in threw itself up. This is the harsh reality of a metro that no one comes to help you in a situation like this. You are all alone and left for dying.

I supported myself on nearby walls to keep myself erect. There was a tornado in my stomach as well as my head. Another round of heaving happened I closed my eyes. Even breathing was getting difficult now. The irritating smell of poison was nauseating me. I heard a familiar voice. It was Sid.

"You okay Rahul? And what is this white spot?" Sid said. There was constant white lather coming out of my mouth which I wiped through the hanky, which was fully wet till now.

"I'm okay" I said although it was sounding as i-a-m-o-k. Any idiot in this world would have easily guessed that something has happened, even SId. He dialled Yash's cell although I was resisting. In almost no time Viks and Yash were there. By this time I had told Sid what happened, mostly in broken sentences and gesticulation.

"Why?" Viks shouted at me with his full energy though kind as Sid told him. He was looking most stressed among us. I'm sure he wanted to say many things but was hurried and worried. I kept quiet rather couldn't say anything.

"Walk fast. Let's not delay" Viks held me and pulled me.

We hired a taxi. "To the nearest hospital." Viks said as we sat inside. I was feeling numb and couldn't sense what was happening around me. Yash was rubbing my back to give me some relief. Viks was waving a red hanky outside the window, a sign of emergency. Nearby vehicles gave us pass and even traffic police didn't make us stop at the signals.

"My dad is a doctor. Let's go to his hospital" Sid said.

"No" I said.

"It would be better if we keep our parents away from this or else he could be in trouble" Yash said.

'EMERGENCY WARD-DHAKURIA MEDICAL COLLEGE AND HOSPITAL' was the board near which the taxi driver stopped. Viks was doing things really actively. He went to the counter, filled the form, and completed the other formalities in no time. A doctor arrived soon to see me.

He peeped into my eyes with a blue torch. He put his stethoscope to check heart beat. Then he checked by blood pressure followed by pulse check.

"What happened to him?" He asked

"He took wrong medicine by mistake" Viks replied.

"What have you taken?" He asked. Yash gave him the bottle.

"This is a strong poison. And you've taken good amount also" He said examining the empty bottle.

Now what was good amount? Good amount meant safe amount or good enough to make me reach heaven? Well, I don't know. And I didn't want to know. Life and death didn't mean anything to me at that moment.

"What was the reason?" He asked.

"I know you guys. It must be either examination or girls" He replied himself.

"No Sir. It was an accident. He took the medicines by mistake" Yash said. We had no choice except lying. Telling the truth might have made it a huge issue. And I didn't want that. I didn't want Sonia to get into any sort of trouble. For this reason only I didn't write any suicide letter before taking it in.

"It will be a police case. Go to the nearest police station and get FIR done"

"Sir. We can't get FIR so quickly, please admit him now. I'll get FIR in some time."

"No. It's against the rules. We can't admit without FIR in cases like this."

"Please sir. We are students. We don't have anybody out here." Yash said.

"Where do you study?" He asked.

"Sir we study engineering in JU"

"JU? Students of JU and you do these silly things?" He said. Even after many attempts of ours he didn't believe that it was by mistake.

These people were too experienced.

"I'm trying to arrange a bed for you on special quota." He said and went to the registration section. Ah! The reputation of JU hit somewhere finally.

"If we do FIR, then police will come and this matter will get spread everywhere, even in your family." Yash said.

"No. Please..........not family please....." It was really difficult to speak

"But without FIR they won't do anything. Let's see if we can find a loophole" Viks said.

This time there was blood outside my mouth. Things were getting worse.

"You get bed number 218" He said and brought a stretcher to carry me. I was riding it for the first time.

As I was lying on bed number 218 Viks came with a lady doctor. I saw he was working very hard.

The doctor was around 25, newly pass-out probably. She re-examined me with stetho and BP machine and handed over a list of medicines and injections and other stuffs to Yash saying "get these".

The list was about ten inches long. I peeped to see what was written on the paper but everything was written in Code Words which only doctors write and chemists read. One thing I observed was the list was containing about twenty items at least. I got afraid thinking of what they would do with me.

When Yash arrived, she resumed her work. She tore the packet on which it was printed RYLE'S TUBE. She applied some gel on tube's one end and started inserted the pipe into my nose. It was damn hurting. My nose started bleeding badly. I doubted if she was following the correct procedure or not. Probably I was her first patient. These government hospitals do give away the patients in the hands of interns or worse maybe she was of reserved quota.

She jerked the tube into my nose, harder this time and it bled with the flow of Ganges. My yellow T shirt became partly orange with red blood.

With the corner of my tearful eyes I saw Sid crying. He was a kid after all. How could he stand this much?

"I'm going to call dad" Sid said.

"Ya maybe he could help us" Viks said.

"But Rahul could get in trouble then" Yash said.

"Ya that is true but his life is more important" Viks said. By this time the quack gave up and went to wash her blood red hands. She didn't even wear gloves.

"Let's shift him to some other hospital" Sid said.

"It would take too long to take him to other hospital plus we'd again be facing problems in getting him admitted there, the same FIR stuffs and all" Viks said.

"I have an idea. We'll just tell his dad that one of our friends is ill. Just recommend us a good doctor in this hospital. He must be having sources and contacts in this hospital too." Yash said.

They went to call from a coin-phone which was hanging outside the emergency ward. Sid inserted one rupee coin inside.

"I can't hear anything" Sid said.

"The phone is dead" Viks said as he took the receiver of the phone from Sid. Even the phone was dead in this hospital. I doubted the abilities of the hospital.

A senior doctor arrived. He was also young, maybe in early 30s, but his glowing face exhibited intelligence. He came after Sid's dad called him up and he took immediate action with his assistants. They fitted the tube inside my nose and sucked whatever poison was inside my stomach through the pipe. They injected some powdered charcoal solution into my stomach through the same tube. Charcoal absorbs organic solvents, I read in chemistry. They put a channel on my hand through which bottle of saline was injected. The saline was being injected continuously to irrigate my body system.

"What happened to him?" The doctor asked. Everyone was asking the same questions and we were also giving same replies. I moved a little out of discomfort.

"Keep lying" The doctor said but don't know to whom; was it for me or them? The doctor left soon, he must be having a busy schedule. Viks followed him to ask something. They all did everything in pretty fast time; it was just a little more than an hour till now. I closed my eyes out of dizziness and don't know when I fell asleep.

I was totally numb, too shocked even to cry. My head was heavy and I was feeling sleepy. I was feeling very tired and strange animated sounds were coming from my stomach.

I got up after twelve hours straight, I found many wirings and fluid system circuits attached to me. The howling of a patient's parents, who had just died, brought me out of sleep. I saw many other patients lying beside me, someone bleeding, someone crying, big machines were fitted to someone. Hospital is the place which makes you feel that you're really among one of them, ill, standing next to death. I was watching these by moving only eyes but my head was still. But where the hell were Sid, Viks and Yash?

I moved my eyes towards the entrance and what I saw just froze me. Tiwari uncle was entering the room followed by aunty and Vishal.

How did he come to know about me being hospitalised? I closed my eyes, like ostrich, hoping they wouldn't see me. And if they saw me it would be my end.

Even after two minutes when no one came near me, I opened my eyes. I sighed with relief I saw them sitting beside another patient, bed no 322, diagonally opposite to me. So they came to see another patient. They brought a bouquet of flowers for the patient. I suppose the bouquet serves two purposes:-(a) If the patient gets well then it was a gift. (b) And if the patient dies, then for the instant funeral.

I turned myself to different side so that they couldn't recognise me. It took a lot of effort to turn with those pipes fitted in me.

Fifteen minutes later I heard them going. "Get well soon" He said and moved towards the door. I heard their foot-steps fade and they finally got out the room and I was safe. Ah! What a relief.

Suddenly the intelligent donkey of the house 'Vishal' shouted in his sound-bomb voice "Mummy , papa. See it's Rahul bhaiya there" He probably saw me through the window.

The family rushed into the room and surveyed from above. Uncle said "Rahul! You're here? What has happened to you?"

"Nothing uncle. Just a small accident" I couldn't tell how much it was hurting to open my mouth and speak. The pipe through the nose was constantly hitting the trachea. But if I didn't talk, it would appear more serious. Where the hell were Sid, Yash and Viks?

"It can't be a small accident. You look seriously ill. So many pipes are here and there" Aunty said.

He asked compounder and he told him "it's case of poisoning"

"Poison?" Aunty shouted almost fading.

They asked me the question we were tired answering and I kept unchanged on the reply. Uncle and Aunty got out for something, I don't know what.

Vishal asked "How does it feel? I saw this in TV. " He was excited to see all this. He held a pipe and moved his hand along with the pipe which ended with the needle on my hand. It ached.

"How many injections did u get?" He asked watching the needle. I was feeling like pulling his hair and slapping him.

"How did the poison taste?"

Better than your mom's food, I wanted to say but I remained silent to all the questions.

"Will you live?" This question brought my heart to a standstill. When you take poison you feel nothing but when it comes to dying you're really afraid and so was I.

Meanwhile Uncle and Aunty returned with the doctor, the lady doctor. I got more frightened.

"Your nani knows all this or not?" Uncle said and called nani from his cellphone. He told nani the whole story which compounder and doctor had told him.

"What happened beta?" Nani was screaming in a terrible pitch. Who needs speaker phone when nani was talking at opposite side?

These news spread like forest fire. Fifteen minutes and my whole dynasty started calling.

"Kring Kring" the cellphone ranged. But. This wasn't my ringtone. This was Sid's ringtone. How did my relatives get Sid's number? I opened my eyes and there was Sid's standing. But where were Uncle Aunty and Vishal?

"How are you feeling now? You were sleeping since last afternoon. It's been almost twenty two hours" Sid said. Oh! So it was a nightmare rather daymare.

"Where are Viks and Yash?" I asked

"They went back. Only one attendant can be with patient after nine"

During the class hours Viks and Yash sat with me alternatively and Sid attended classes. They never talked about any serious topics and just shared jokes to keep the mood light. Rest of the time Sid was a good nurse owing to his feminine character and the knowledge of basics of medical sciences from his father. He adjusted those pipes when it was required and constantly replaced saline. The biggest problem I faced while bearing those elephant trunks was going to toilet. He even took me to the toilet carrying those bottles in his hand.

"Look that side" I told to him when I was inside and the door couldn't be locked because of pipes.

I had all the free time in the hospital to see the surroundings of hospital. Many patients died in front of me. And the dead Coin-phone definitely gave profit to the hospital as it gulped many ‡ one rupee coins of the people.

Meanwhile I was shifted from emergency ward to general ward, meaning the chance of emergency mishap was over and I was safe. They kept me admitted for last one day to observe the stability or something like that. I hadn't bathed for last two days and felt like Viks.

The doctor arrived for the daily check up next morning. He removed the pipes and channels and all. He checked my BP and heart beat and said "You are okay now. We may discharge you. But before that I want to know the truth. I know it wasn't an accident as you are telling." He paused and said "What happened exactly? Was it because of girl?"

We lowered our eyes and stood quiet. Sometimes silence speaks everything.

"Okay. One of you, come with me" he said.

He should have understood. He was young too and must have been through this phase. He gave us the discharge certificate or the exit pass without which we couldn't leave the hospital. Thankfully he discharged me without asking for FIR.

Sweet Revenge

We tried to curb the matter among ourselves only, but these matters hardly get clogged inside a room. Though everyone did not know, but many did. Every day someone or the other came asking "I heard you were in hospital. Girlfriend betrayed you?" It was like an open secret but we still tried making some new stories. Many people showed sympathy "Oh! I'm sorry for you. Don't worry you'll get a better girl". And it felt very sick when somebody took pity on me "Let him take the seat if he wants. You know he is sad". And it felt even sicker when you came to know that a person was treating with you very politely out of sympathy.

And there was another group of people who thought me a psycho. They were afraid of my erratic nature and started staying away from me as if I'd kill them.

Unsuccessful suicide attempt is like a curse. It doesn't kill your physical body, but it kills your soul. I hoped that I had died. Even 3 days of hospital changes your lifestyle hugely.

The world around us also doesn't make it easy. They keep asking you unanswerable questions. Some asked every minute details of how-it-happened and reminded me of the worst time of my life. What did they want, to listen to some spicy talk? I just wanted to be left alone at my stage which was miserable enough. Then there was Sid "You didn't care about your parents before doing such things? They care so much about you. They took your care from your childhood and when you got young you did this for a girl. Shame on you" I had to listen even to an idiot like Sid. I didn't say a word in reply. I didn't have a word. What would I say? That I didn't have parents and they didn't care about me and I didn't care about them.

Smitten I was. How much I loved her and what I got in return - Betrayal. I was feeling cheated. So my life meant nothing to her. Was she playing with me? (Although 'playing with me' phrase is girls' patent but it was okay in today's modern world).

One day I opened my Orkut account which I couldn't check for last four days. No. of scraps was the same as before, which meant no one had scrapped me in last few days, sad. I opened her profile after that which I had bookmarked because I had to visit it so often. The first few scraps were her friends' asking about notes and all and casual hi-s and bye-s. Then I scrolled to the end of page and then the next page. And what I saw there, shocked me more than 440 volts could do.

Akshita: I think he did this to gain sympathy.

Rina: He is queen of dramas....rather king :P

Monika: Is the psycho troubling you anymore?

Yes, I was psycho now. Once the girl parts off with a guy then that guy becomes the worst person on this earth for her and her friends.

Piya: There was no poison voison. He was trying to vomit by drinking too much of mirinda.

Romita: Someone is going to die soon....he...he ;)

Rashmi: How was the drama? Did you enjoy? You should have bought popcorn and cold-drinks that would have increased the enjoyment of the show.

Sid was watching these scraps from behind, which I didn't know until he began to laugh loudly holding his mouth. "Drama King"

Idiot always hurts me. He is real idiot, dumb, ass, and blockhead. But maybe I deserved this. He had all the rights to laugh at me.

Sometimes life is not like movies. I mean I expected that Sonia would come back to me when I was on deathbed, but that never happened. I never thought in my worst of the dreams that my image would be that of a Drama king. I mean I was not like Tomoghno and all.

Out of anger I threw my cellphone. No points for guessing what would have happened after that-the display cracked and Sonia's pic which was still the wallpaper of my cellphone splintered. Her face was distorted cracked from here and there. This is what I wanted. To distort her face. Bang her slap. I was burning with the feeling of revenge. I won't leave her. I would destroy her. I would distribute her phone number; write it on the toilet walls of each train I travel in, and print pamphlets and distribute her number with address. Even if she changed her mobile number, I had her landline number. I didn't call on that because generally her mom picked it up. And I had many pics which I took from my cell and the snaps she gave; I wanted to post it randomly here and there on internet. And from their pics make fake videos by picture editor and video editor, what kind of videos you know. And the close pics I had with her, I wanted it to post it to her mom, and showing how much innocent her daughter was. I wanted settling of scores at any cost.

At night when lights were off and I was lying on the bed and just tossing sides Viks asked" What are you thinking? Still thinking of her?"

"Nah." I replied.

"You know if I ever get a chance, I'll ruin that girl Sonia. But there is nothing we can do about it" Viks said.

"Forget all this and sleep." I said and acted to sleep. Had I not done this, this discussion would have taken the whole night. Viks also slept after a few minutes. But I was lost in my thoughts for hours and hours.

Suddenly an idea flickered into my mind. Good ideas always come when you are in toilet or you're sleeping, see Archimedes, see Newton. What did I want? I wanted to ask Sonia why she did this. I wanted to talk to her for one hour and even if forcibly. But her friends wouldn't let me talk and even Sonia wouldn't talk to me. So someway I'd have to create a situation where we two could talk alone and Ya Sonia shouldn't run away..

I'm not that lucky that I'd someday get stuck in rain with Sonia together under the same shed. And she would have no option of running away. But, this was real life. So what should I do? What if...what if kidnap her up and then talk to her?

"Viks. Get up. Get up Viks. I have got an idea" "What idea?" he said half sleeping.

"What if we capture Sonia?"

"Capture. What do you mean?"

"Capture means we will capture her from somewhere into a car or something." I didn't want to use the word kidnap as it sounded dodgy and dangerous.

"Sleep now and let me sleep. We will talk about this tomorrow" He was very sleepy. Once Viks sleeps he almost dies. But my eyes were wide open and shining very brightly.

Throughout the night I was thinking about this only. What will I do and how. I was making plans on mental maps.

Next morning I told whatever I thought to Viks and he readily agreed. But Yash wasn't agreeing. We had to take the pains of digging thousand mines to make him agree. And Yash was indispensible for the plan as only he knew how to drive a car. Inclusion of anyone else as driver would mean extra complexity in the plan. And Sid, we decided not to tell him a word about this. He was plain dumb and couldn't digest this.

Right from the next day, I started to spy her paths and timings. And I had to bunk all my classes for this. Proxies were saving me from the ghostly professors. I already had the idea of where she went at what time but just for a check I kept noting all these.

Meanwhile my college bag which I carried to the college only twice before, soon got transformed into what we called "daru wala bag". It was the same "R S" bag by the way. The bag brought into our room the bottles quite often, hiding them from the warden and others. And the day after a bottle of white rum cracked and the rum got assimilated into every thread of it, the bag started giving a characteristic smell which brought its name. We rarely thought of washing the bag, thinking that other bottles may rupture too.

In two weeks I got a fair idea of where she went and at what time. I found she crossed a bridge every day at around six pm. And the bridge was deserted, very empty, with no man, no car. Actually it was a shortcut route to her house; it was a lesser used small bridge which was unknown to most of the public. So it was the safest place for us to execute our plan.

Next, Bollywood showed way for us and we booked a car on rent for a whole day and that too on false identity, so that even if something wrong happens we won't be in trouble. Viks arranged a good fake government I-card with false stamps and all with the power of union. We were over-cautious for eliminating every possible mistake. Yash was still very wary of this plan. He said it was not safe and practicable. But I was always pressing him and having Viks on my side did the rest.

And finally the D-day came. We had our booked Maruti OMNI with us. We chose OMNI because it was good for pulling someone in because it has wide sliding doors, as we saw in movies. Yash was to drive the car.

The whole plan was like this. I knew Sonia would cross the bridge between six and six-thirty. And the bridge was generally deserted plus it would be dark so no one could recognise us even if they saw us. And even if someone noted down the car number then also we were safe. We kept a stone for marking a point- when Sonia would cross that point, we'd start our car. We calculated all this with simple kinematic calculations taking many assumptions.

After Sonia would come to the point, we would start the car slowly with headlights off. Move it towards her at around 10 KPH. As soon as we would reach in front of Sonia, Viks will open the car's door and pull her inside and I was ready with hanky inside to keep on her mouth, to suppress her cries(using a clean hanky ofcourse). We had already talked of many precautions which we should take. We shouldn't frighten her; or else she would get down by the stairs, which were at side of the bridge. So we'd have to drive extra cautiously. And we should keep the car at safe distance from the footpath neither too near nor too far to pull her in. And after that we'd raise the window glasses of car which were tinted; we had chosen the car with these specifications.

And when we'd get her inside we should not misbehave with her. We'd first calm her down and then talk to her. And we'd be extra cautious not to hurt her while pulling. Viks would just pull her by hands and I'd pull her rest of the body and we'd talk to her calmly, no display of strong emotions.

After this part of our plan gets successful, we'd go to a park which we knew always remained empty. And after that Viks and Yash would leave and I and Sonia would talk inside the locked car.

"I'm feeling frightened" Yash said while we were waiting inside our car at the pre-decided place. Everything was predefined and planned for today. There was no scope of mistake.

"You are always frightened. C'mon man show some guts. And please don't quit at this stage" I said

"No I'm not quitting. But still I'm getting anxious. I have strong apprehension that something bad will happen today"

"Keep your bloody mouth shut. Everything will happen correctly as per the plan. Anyways you don't have to do much. Just drive the car properly and we'll manage the rest." Viks said.

"See is she coming?" Yash whispered seeing a girl coming from the dark. Yes she was Sonia, I recognised. I noticed that there was no vehicle or any person other than us on the bridge. Bloody lucky I was.

Sonia was walking on the footpath of the bridge. She was wearing kurti and jeans whose colours I couldn't tell as it was fairly dark by then. She was walking with her eyes digging the ground, as she always did. Why she always looked down and not straight. I was planning this much and she was walking, looking almost lost in herself biting her lips. Anyways it made our work easier.

As Sonia walked to the marked spot, Yash started the car. Viks raised his thumbs for wishing us luck. I was very panicky as now she was less than fifty metres distance. With our car crawling at ten KPH, I guessed we'd get her in roughly twenty seconds.

Just twenty seconds and I'd be talking to her after so many days. I'd talk to her about everything. I would first scold her and then forgive her. I heard kissing is the best way to remind the girl of the relationship. I would kiss her and...and I would gift her favourite chocolate, which I had inside my bag to hide from Yash and Viks. I would do this. I would do that. Ten seconds passed while I was thinking this.

Ten more seconds and Sonia would be with me. I would express all my emotions. Would tell her that how much I missed her each moment. I'd make her remember of our relation times. I'd make her remind of our first kiss, first official date, dharma bhrahsta and many other things. I'd cry in her lap. She would also get emotional and come back to me. She will have to. How much I loved her. How much risk I took in doing all this. I was telling everyone that I hated her, but from my inside I couldn't hate her, though I should have.

Now the countdown was starting. Sonia was about twenty metres away. Viks and I were prepared for our jobs. All eyes were set on the movement of Sonia. Each second was passing very much stretched as if time had dilated. A few more milliseconds and we'd open the doors and pull Sonia in. I was preparing my mind for last moment adjustments. Yash was sweating out of anxiousness.

Now I could see that Sonia was wearing blue kurti and gray jeans. And she was wearing the big earrings which I used to call bangle earrings. I would be playing with those earrings again after a few moments.

Suddenly we heard a bursting sound and our car wobbled and Yash braked to stop the car. And in haste Yash grabbed the steering hard and ended up honking the horn.

Meanwhile Sonia sensed something and got down the bridge with the ladder quickly, which was in the side of the bridge to get down the bridge in between. Afterall it was 6:30 and she was walking alone on a lonely bridge. A car's sudden stopping and honking was enough to frighten her. The game of snake and ladder was over, Sonia got the ladder and we were bitten by the snake. Atleast she didn't see any of us.

New Life

"What happened Yash. Why did you stop suddenly? Any problem in car or what?" Viks asked.

Even after such a tremendous plan such a stupid thing spoiled it. How it could happen? Why did it get punctured at that moment of time? Maybe destiny too didn't want this to happen. Frustrated we called a mechanic, got the puncture repaired and drove back to the place from where we rented the car. Then we returned to hostel by bus.

"What to do now? We will have to go tomorrow for our incomplete plan. " I said in the night when we three were sitting near the pond of the hostel. I reached half an hour after Viks and Yash as I went to eat in the canteen. They were already discussing something.

"Tomorrow again?" Yash said with the face like a rotten mango.

"Why? What is problem with tomorrow? If you tried today, you can do it tomorrow also" I said.

"No. I am way too afraid. I was trembling today; I just can't do it tomorrow." Yash said.

"C'mon phattu, one last time. Everything will work correctly this time" I insisted again.

"NO" He shouted. "Sorry whatever you think, My answer is no. And I'm serious this time" I shivered with the impact of his shout.

"Tell him Viks. Make him understand." I turned to Viks. Only he was the one who could control the situation. Last time also, he only made Yash agree. "Viks say something" But hey! Why was Viks quiet? Did Viks also change his mind?

"Rahul...Listen man. Please just listen. Understand our stands also." He said 'our'. He was taking Yash's side. He continued very calmly "We tried to help you. We did na? Even if it was so risky. We tried our level best."

"Risky? It was not risky. It was well planned...considering all the safety measures"

"It was very risky *yaar*. You don't know"

"How? It was so easy"

"Okay even if we take your words. If everything went correctly, what would you do after that? After getting Sonia in?"

"I would...I would have talked to her...and asked her...many things"

"What do you think; she would have talked to you?"

"Ofcourse. Did she have any other option?"

"Take my words she would not talk to you. And who knows she could even tell her parents about this and lodge a police complaint against you"

"She would never do that. I know her. And after talking to me, everything would have sorted out"

"Don't live in fool's paradise. How can you be so sure about the girl who left you dying?" Viks said almost scolding me. I lowered my eyes. Maybe he was speaking the harsh truth.

"And you know what. Women in India have got enormous legal powers. Even their smallest complaint can ruin your career. One FIR and you will be ruined forever. Even if the allegation is false." Viks continued.

"If you knew this much then why did you do it first time?" I asked.

"I was carried away with emotions. Now when I get the time to think and I think, I see the risk involved." Viks said and stopped.

"We know you still love her. There is nothing wrong in that. We even know about your whole operation dog thing" Yash said.

Shit! How come they know about my operation dog? I kept it top secret and I shift+deleted it.

"You forget that the shift key was not functioning. So when you shift deleted the senti-mail, it went to recycle bin and we read it from there" Viks said. I felt embarrassed and ashamed.

"I know we are getting a bit harsh on you but.....try to forget her, you don't have any other option. Accept the reality, she would never come back." Viks again.

Just because they didn't want to help me, they were telling me to forget her. No way. I'll not let this happen.

"Look *yaar*, you are not the first guy who is facing these things. These things happen to everyone. Ninety percent of love story doesn't materialise. Just take it easy. There is a lot more to do in life" Yash said.

"These things do happen. These are ups and downs of life. Take it casually. So be practical. You have to go a long way in life. And trust me she was not a good girl for you. There are plenty of other fishes in the sea. Go and catch them." Yash said.

"Rather I would say you are lucky enough that you got over with her, coz if she left you now, she could have left you later also and that would have been more painful for you. If she was this kind of girl then consider yourself to be lucky enough to get rid of her soon. God saved you from that bitch" Viks said.

"I...I" Words were not coming of my mind. I was on the verge of emotional breakdown. I got up from there as I didn't want to cry in front of them and then ran to the terrace. There I took the darkest corner. It was winter starting in Kolkata and the terrace was vacant. In any other season the terrace used to be flooded with guys talking to their girlfriends. I broke into cry and whimpered.

Yes, Viks and Yash were telling the truth. She would never come back to me. I had lost her forever. I sobbed and sobbed till my head ached to the point of bursting and the tear stocks were ending. I felt my body was getting hot and feverish. The tears had made my cheek shin very rough. My right nose was also blocked.

I tried to divert my mind from these topics. I did the best I could do. What we can do if we can't get them into our life? Even after expressing all our vehement emotions. We can't force them.

Love is a sacrifice. I was accepting the fact that there was no way she could come back. Sometimes we have to give up at some point of time. I was wondering why I was thinking about sacrifice and all at 12 in the night. Did I get crazy and had lost my mental balance?

I will forget her. I'll have to forget her. For this I will have to shift+delete the past one year from my life. I started with her SMSes, there were lot of them-I love you, Missing you..all fake SMSes. I deleted all of them. I deleted her number, which was now permanently switched off or changed. I decided to erase all the mementoes. I also deleted her scraps from Orkut and chats that I had stored.

"I will return her stuffs-the earrings, her school snaps and many other things. I will return everything that reminded me of her." I thought.

Suddenly I realised that I had many other things in life. There were many pending tasks. I was busy in doing all the foolish things and thinking of her all the day. I had many goals in life. I had to gear up for this year's fest. I didn't want to be late like last time and be unprepared for the competition. We had to find a band or form a new one. By the way I should mention here that Night rockers band dismantled after a week after last Sanskriti. It had to. We had several issues. Things were not going the way we wanted to. Every relation gets broken up, what was a band?

Next day Vishal called on my cell "Bhaiya. You haven't come here since so many days. Please come na"

Ya it was true I hadn't been there since two months. First I was busy being depressed, then DMCH and then planning for you know what.

"I'll come tomorrow" I told him.

I went downstairs to my room and made a new yahoo mail account for mailing Sonia. I suspected that she had blocked my main e-mail id. I mailed her

"Hey there,

Here's no prank. I want to return your stuffs, your earrings, snaps and all.....they don't mean anything to me now. Take them back. I'll get these items in a bag on Friday 12th at 2 pm, PCB. Come if you want to take them. Or else I'll throw these in dumps.

Your enemy, Rahul"

"You came after so many days beta?" Aunty said as I reached there.

"Aunty I was busy in semesters, projects, tests and all" I said casually. I had not to show, how much depressed I was. And elders never questioned us whenever we told them that we were busy in projects. We only knew how many projects we actually did.

"Wait I'm getting you something to eat" Aunty said and went to the kitchen. She always wanted to see me eating.

"How are you bhaiya?" Vishal came running. He saw his prey.

"Have you heard of the latest Microsoft game..." I cut his dialogue in between and asked changing the topic "Who is playing drums?" I knew if Vishal got started then he won't stop and I'll have to discuss about those crappy computer games in which I was least interested. And sound of drum fascinated me. It inspired me to make our new band.

"He is Shibhashish da. He is from your college only. He plays very well. He also plays in a band" Vishal replied.

"Can we meet him?" I asked. I wanted to meet this guy. He might be of some help.

"Ofcourse. He stays on the first floor. He is a very good bhaiya"

We rung the call bell and Shibashish's mom opened the door and told us to sit on the sofa.

"Hi dada. See he is Shibhashish da. He was the one who was playing drums. He is expert drummer and plays in a band"

I saw him and he saw me and he shouted "What are you doing here in my home?"

I tried to recall his face, where did I see him? It was.....it was....Oh Shit! He was the Shiba, the one whom I had beaten like drum.

"Do you know each other? He is also from your college" Vishal asked.

"Yes I know him very well. Can I talk to him in private for a minute Vishal?" Shiba said. Vishal agreed.

"How dare you enter my house and how do you know Vishal? And why have you come here?" He said when Vishal left.

"Vishal is my cousin. I heard your drums when I was in their house. And we came here to see the man behind it. You play really well"

"Get out from here just now. I don't want to fight with you here; I don't want my parents to know all this. We'll resolve this matter in college. You just buzz off"

He pushed me outside his house and shut the door hard on me. What else could I expect?

"What were you both talking?" Vishal asked when we reached his house.

"Nothing. Just about college stuffs" I replied.

I heard a weeping voice. I went to see that Aunty was sobbing there in front of TV. Why was she crying? Did she see any of the touching episodes of saas bahu?

"Hey aunty! Why are you crying?"

"No one cares for me. See, no one even bothers to remember my birthday, neither your uncle nor your brother. No one"

"What do they think of me? Am I just their maid who works for them day and night. Cleans room, washes clothes and cooks food." When women start non-stop blabbering, don't stop them. Let them do so. It relieves them a lot. Just listen to them and half the problem would be solved.

"Let your Uncle come from office today. I'll show who I am. I will stop doing house hold work. And from now on I'm not going to cook"

"Yes aunty! Yes! Please quit cooking" I said in my mind.

Aunty kept telling her sorrows to me till next half an hour or so after which Uncle came. This was the start of Battle of Dum Dum – II. Same torn pillows, rotten tomatoes, sound bombs, books, boxes were weapons. The cause of fight kept changing, as usual. Aunty pledged that she would stop cooking. Uncle ordered the food from restaurant for celebrating Aunty's birthday and to cool her down.

After waking up from the afternoon nap, I missed her the most. I stopped going to the arts faculty side, but my eyes were always searching her in the crowd, one glimpse, just one glimpse. But we hardly ever saw each other; we had different paths and timings.

Many songs reminded me of her like Tere Bin, Doorie, Kuch Is tarah; and I played these songs over and over again, which gave me a weird and wonderful feeling that she was with me. It relieved me a little, though it was a temporary effect. I believe music and memory have some basic root relation. Whenever you hear the same songs, you are carried by time machine to the same time; the time when you were happy and were playing this song on your cell, sitting hands in hands with her - the good old time. Every time I tried forgetting her but just couldn't remember to forget her.

And talking of mobile, my speed dial 3 was empty. I didn't put any other number on speed dial 3.

But I had to forget her permanently. And for this I would have to stop listening to those songs and return her belongings to her.

I went to my room and opened my big suitcase. I was lucky Viks was not in the room, as he had to go to GB or general body meet of college union. With him in room, doing all this would have been difficult and weird. I started taking out the materials out of the overstuffed box. All my dirty clothes were lying inside it wrinkled, rolled and stinky. Then came out the diary in which I had her snaps. I always kept her things very carefully. There were some ten snaps in the diary. I took a big polybag and put the photos into it. A pebble which I collected at birla palneteriam, as a memory of our first offcial date. Then came the earrings which she gave, the last day we met before going to vacation. Her gifts and other things. There were lots of them. Whatever thing I found having potential to remind me of her, I bagged in the polybag. What they were now, just scraps, a last few scraps of love.

The polybag became very full. I stapled it so that things don't come out of it. I gave a check again if anything of her was left or not. No, there was nothing in the suitcase. But as I opened the diary a five hundred rupee note fell on the ground. Oh! That was the same five hundred which was returned by the puppy shop, when I returned the puppy of operation dog. But I had stapled the polybag and it was a thick one. I didn't want to keep it as it was also a memento of her. I thought of giving it to some poor people as charity money. But should I give it to others what I kept for her? No, I should give it to her afterall it was her birthday gift. But I knew she wouldn't take as such. Should I open the staples? Or should I do something else with it. Should I give her something worth 500. But she won't take any gift or anything. The bulb glowed in my mind when I thought what could one do with exact five hundred. An advertisement clicked in my mind "500-get your connection lifetime". Yes this was the solution. I will ez-recharge on her old cell no. And make it a lifetime. A simple and silent gift, which she couldn't deny. And the number would be the only living sign of our dying relationship and I wanted it to keep it living forever.

I was walking to the PCB at sharp two pm. I never had been more punctual ever in my life. I was walking hastily to the place. I had plugged iPod into my ears and was playing in full sound "I've become so numb-linkin park number" to keep me engaged and distracted from the seriousness of what I was doing. And there she was standing with Monica. I reached the place. I didn't look her face. I knew that would make me weak. My mind was shouting "this is the chance. Go and talk to her". But I didn't stop. I just threw the polybag containing the stuffs on that on the platform where we used to sit. The next moment I turned and walked pacing. I didn't turn back again and moved straight. Yes! I did it. I did it successfully.

I can't explain the power of giving up things. It makes feel so relieved. The path the saints showed us. It feels as if all the problems were solved. You get above all the problems. And the numb song was suiting the situation. I was becoming numb.

The numb track was over and other song started "what I've done-linkin park again". There are times when you feel, realise and react five minutes after you have finished everything. What I had done? I had returned her everything. That was the last nail in the coffin of our relationship. I myself closed all the gates of her coming back. I lost her forever. This was the end. Tears showered from my eyes as a momentary impact. I don't know why, at this moment, whatever happened between me and Sonia was playing again in my videographic memory. The moments we enjoyed, the happy days. And she even wrote a testimonial for me in form of a mail-the testimail.

The testimail

I didn't write a testi on orkut coz I thought that everything won't fit within 1024 characters....so it's better I write testi in form of a mail........testimail....well I'm too confused....from where to start n where to end.....

First of all I take u as my friend n then my love.....I feel that in any relationship, friendship is the most imp thing.....n I can say that you're my best friend coz u know many things about me n understand me so much, which no one could ever do.....

We've known each other for quite some time now....initially you were this idiotic guy who never got a copy to college n borrowed paper from others....still remember that dumb photography class n how we met.....n I used to think that my God.....he's such a nonstop chatter box....when does he keep his mouth shut???Then gradually when I got to know u more, my thoughts changed n we became close friends.... I knew u as jus a good friend who's there to help me whenever I need and is there to solve my problems and be my support......sometimes you can be really childish n irritating, n since I get irritated too soon, it's all the more good for you.....You're like 19 year old kid who loves to throw tantrums.

During a phase of life, I was going through a very hard time....coz it's not easy and I wish that no one should ever go through that phase of life......you were there with me as a very strong support...don't know why...but I used to feel very relieved aft talking to you or even after crying in front of you.....and all the similarities brought us closer to each other.....especially the greatest coincidence...which was more like a shock for both of us...rather than a surprise.....

And I remember the way you proposed me. Those jumpy eyes, shaky legs, nervous face and the stammered "I don't know about you but I like you", you were looking so cute! Your overall appearance that day induced laughter and my happiness added more to it. And I deliberately made you more nervous by asking "like? In what ways?" and you were looking like you'd faint and fall down ~~just now~~ right then.

I'm happy with u and I want to spend the rest of my life happily with u.....ya if you want extramarital then you can do...I won't mind........just kidding....I'll kill you if you do that.........but I really hope that we remain happy like this forever.....fights n misunderstandings happen in every relationship....but neither of us should drag it n spoil the situation all the more....we've gone through our hard times too.....but it should always be within a limit....love should be like....you expect the other person to know what you've to say before you open your mouth to say it....and compromises should always be both sided....or else there's always *a feeling that "I did this for you and what did u do?" I hope I'm not getting too philosophical...don't worry I never had that subject.....*

Anyways leave all that.....now let's talk about something else.....your negative points...I HATE it when you sing Atif's songs.....coz no one can sing it the way he does.....n you're nowhere near to Atif Aslam...got it? secondly you're too short....my mom will say that too......you kiss too hard....and loads of many more things......but overall you're a sweetheart.....n I love u a lotttttttttt....more than my life....always keep your trust in me n love me like this forever......coz no matter what but I can never lie to u about anything or anyone n I want you to do the same too

It's enough for today....my hands are aching now.... I'll write more later....Mom is calling for lunch....

Love you.....take care

Mmmmmmmmmmmmmmmmmmmmmmmuuuuuuuuuuuuuuuuuuuuuuuuuuuaaaaaaaaaaaaaaaaaaaaaahhhhhhhhhhhhhh

Lal Kothi

I knew it was over. I had given up. It was the time to take my life forward; face the reality; live it without her. She won't be coming back ever. It was the time to forget her. Take her out of my mind. And I was doing this. And it was so kind of Yash and Viks who fully understood my situation and always kept me engaged in one thing or other. They never left me alone, never let me feel lonely. They always kept me happy and tolerated my unnecessary crabbiness.

In semesters also Yash and Viks helped me a lot. Also Sid, who provided me his colourful notes and cleared my doubts.

A month passed. Semester ended. We planned to go to the local Goa-Digha on a Dil-Chahta-Hai trip. We had a huge debate on whether we should take Sid with us or not but finally Sid won.

"Oh! Did I mention, what happened between me and Shiba. The day after I went to his house, he was so worried. He met me in college yesterday. He wanted me to keep my mouth shut about what happened that day in college, on that football match day. He didn't want to be ill-famed in his locality. He probably didn't tell his parents that he got beaten in college. So he wanted to curb the matter. He asked me to keep this matter to myself." I told in the bus.

"Tch tch tch. Poor creepy fellow" Viks said.

"Hey I've got an idea. It is low on moral standards but still it's for our profit. You told that Shiba was a member of band. So he must be having links. Why not you ask him this favour in return. You tell him to help us find us band and we'll keep our mouth shut. If not then...you keep going Dum Dum na" Yash said.

"But this is blackmailing and it's not good" Sid said.

"Everything which profits you is good in this modern world" Viks said.

We reached Digha in five hour or so. We booked a room in a hotel and went straight to the beach. It was sunrise time. We were mesmerised by the beauty of the redness of the sun. Cool breeze was making us shiver. We dipped our feet in the water. It was very cold and so was the sand on which we were standing. We came back to hotel and slept(all three on the same bed and sharing the same blanket)

We got up at around 11 am when it was sunny. Then we went to the beach for taking the bath. Viks didn't want to come into the water but we pulled him in. We had an hour long bath. We played water polo and had swimming race and many other things.

Bathing in sea water was really tiring, I realised this when we came out. Hungry like dogs we ran to the hotel. There were varieties of sea food there, but I being a vegetarian didn't eat them. Viks, Yash and Sid did. After the lunch we bought whiskey that too in black as it was dry day there.

We drank to our brim, except Sid who tasted it for the first time.

Poor Sid, the topper fell in bad company with us. After being loaded, Viks had this very bad habit of taking my phone and dialling any random number and talking. And wasting my balance. And Yash was after my last packet of cigarette as his stocks were over. These two things were the costliest item for me-my balance in cellphone and last packet of cigarette. Take everything else but dare not touch these. Don't know when again we started snoozing after having blabbering arguments and fights.

In the evening, Yash brought another idea very which was eerie indeed. I didn't know why we were doing this. Maybe because of curiosity or frustration or what, I didn't know. Well we were going to red light zone of Digha, the pros house or brothel.

I was afraid of only two things, police and AIDS. The former was still manageable with bribe but the latter was really deadly. And the worst of dying of AIDS is that when you die, you also kill your own and the reputation of the whole family. I mean what would parents think? And those relatives, they will make the last days of our life worse than hell.

"Where are we going? Do you know the place?" I asked after we had walked for about fifteen minutes.

"Lal Kothi" Yash said.

"What is this?"

"A pros-house you fool. Where else did we decide to go?"

"How can you be so certain? Have you ever been here before?"

"Sources my boy. Sources. So you all ready for a great night? We will be having fun" Yash said.

"No. I don't want paid sex" Viks interrupted.

"But what's the problem. I mean.." Yash said.

"No means no. I told about this before also, if you remember"

Viks can be, at times quite firm at his decisions.

"But then why are you coming with us?"

"Just to see the system. You should have the experience of everything in life"

The roads were like French curves. After a lot of twists and turns we arrived "Lal Kothi"

We stood outside the gate for the last moment planning.

A bicycle stopped near us and the rider got down. He took out a plastic bag which was hanging on the handle of cycle and went inside.

"Come inside" The man at the counter waved his hand. A dinosaur like dog was tied with chain at the entrance with a thick chain. We walked slowly to the counter.

"Can we get aaa......" Yash started.

"Yes" He nodded.

"Rs. 200 for short and 800 for the whole night" The man said. He was around forty-five and was looking very rude and stubborn.

"Can't we see girls first?" Yash asked.

"You'll be charged Rs hundred for watching the girls. And that would be non refundable."

"Will these hundred rupees be adjustable? I mean if someone does"

"Yes" The man used the minimum words as if words were also costing.

Without thinking we went to see the girls. And I was standing beside real prostitutes. I mean those bad girls. There were ten of them. Fat, wearing revealing clothes, overstuffed make-up anyone could recognise them. And the place had the smell of strong perfume or itr. The girls smirked as they saw us. I was feeling awful about these girls.

"Go Rahul" Yash murmured.

"You go first" I murmured in returned. We kept doing, you go, you go to each other.

"I will go" I heard a voice. It was none other than the topper of our class.

"What? You..." I was startled. His topper attitude followed here also.

"With which girl" The manager asked. Sid pointed towards one.

"I will not go. I can't do anything so cheap" I said to Yash.

"Me too" Yash replied.

We were waiting outside the room when Sid was inside. Don't know how Sid would be doing and why did he choose this? It was a really bad thing and he shouldn't have done this. Somewhere I was feeling we all were guilty for first getting him to Digha and second taking him to this place. Sid is a kid and can't take judicious decisions. We should have stopped him.

But I was ashamed of myself and was regretting why I came here. And was afraid that if anybody comes to know about this thing and if it leaks out it would be so bad. But Yash assured that Sid won't sneak as he himself was involved. Rest others had confidence on each other.

"What did you do? What things happened" Yash asked excitedly when Sid came out.

"I kissed her" Sid said.

"and what"

"I just kissed her. Rest of the time we were talking. She was so good, so beautiful. I kissed her on her cheeks. I even took her mobile number" Sid said and we all broke into laughter. So he didn't do anything. I felt relieved.

And the funniest thing that happened was Sid went for the HIV test after a week. This was because Viks frightened him, which he loved to do. It was the first test in which he failed. Really Sid was a kid.

Five Months Later

Five months passed like this. Five months was a long time. Many things got changed. I started forgetting Sonia. And we talked to Shiba and he agreed to what we said. We got into our second band – Rustic Devils. We had five months in hand and we practiced rigorously. We were committed to winning this time. Even Orkut got changed and introduced scrapbook lock and album lock and I couldn't see Sonia's scraps and album. Yash elongated his hair and ordered me to have very-short hair with spikes. He was very stylish himself and was making me look stylish too. He was doing all this to give us a cool look like everyone had in bands. I didn't like doing all these show offs but had to listen to Yash's words.

But the biggest change or rather event was happening today. Guess what, Viks was bathing today!!! Believe it or not!!! I was wondering what made him bath, was it the cult fest starting in JU. But he didn't bath in the last two years' fest. Was it because of some other reason? Some big reason. Did Viks make any girlfriend? Bastard will not tell himself. We'll have to spy on him. But! With which soap would Viks bath with? The dettol soap which he bought two years ago, I sometimes used after toilets. That time I thought that the soap was useless, Viks would never need it. But Viks was unaware of this fact and was bathing singing songs. Should I tell him?

"Hey Rahul? All set for today's show?" He said coming out of the bathroom. So it was no use telling him about his soap now. He had already used it, confirmed the smell of dettol. He was standing in his towel with his hair wet. He surely bathed, I still had doubts.

"Yup. This time we'll rock it" I said.

When you don't have anything to lose, you lose all your fear. When you have lost all your fear, all your inhibitions, it gives a Nirvana feeling. Blood rushed into my veins as I got on the stage. I was afraid people would recognise me as the flop singer of last year. But that didn't happen maybe because of our changed look or they simply forgot.

We were to play "Woh Lamhe" of Jal Band. We had practiced very hard this time. I never felt this much charged as if some force was pushing me. I remembered this was the favourite Song of Sonia. While my band members were busy setting their instruments, I ran my eyes into the audience to find that face but couldn't find it. The apparatus got set and I started the song "Na Jane kab se" and Yash played the strings. The audience roared as this was favourite number of many of them. I again tried to find someone. Though my voice was not as half good as Atif but our band made great music. This time there was no booing as last time. Anurag was wonderful on drums and Vinit on keyboard, and you know Yash was the best at guitar.

"Once more" The audience hollered. But we couldn't do it once more. We had to play another song "Smoke on the water". Again we carried off this song really well and I was satisfied with our performance. So were the other band members. Atleast it was not as bad as the last time. Rest the result would tell.

After this we went straight to the food stall. We were damn hungry. And we had to enjoy the rest of the fest. There would be so many events. So many guest artists and so many girls!!! Viks also joined us by this time. We ordered pao bhaji and dosa and chowmein three plates each, at the same time.

The man at the counter raised an eyebrow on us. Wondered how three guys can eat so much. But we were hungry animals and could eat anything then.

While eating I was eyeing the girls around. There were many new faces from different colleges. Some of them were very pretty and gorgeous. Suddenly I turned around to see a known face, not her but Rashmi. She was still smoking and had grown fatter. She was sitting with some people of our college union. She waved hi to Viks and Viks waved in return. How did they know each other? I turned my face other side so that she could not see me. Even if she would have seen me she won't be able recognise me with this spiked looks.

"Who is she? How do you know her?" I asked Viks.

"She is a student of Presidency college. I met her in Nandigram. She is in the same union party in which I am. Just different college but the party is same." Viks replied.

"Girlfriend? You like her?" Yash asked.

"Naah." Viks replied but I saw a hidden twinkle in his eyes. I noticed something fishy.

"That girl is not nice." I said, mainly to Viks. But he was busy exchanging eye messages with her. Then she called him to speak something and he left us. He even left the food, how could he? She was not the right girl for Viks. She had a very long and dirty past of boyfriends, one was Tomoghno.

But hey! What if she talks about me? But why would she? She didn't even know that I was Viks' friend. And she must have forgotten about me, it was a long time back when I met her. And won't they be having any other topic to chat, why would they talk about me?

I enjoyed the rest of the events of the day of fest. But because it was first day of the fest, there were no big events. I saw face painting and participated in some small game sort of events. I went to Yash's flat with him after that. There I opened the website which every youngster opens first before any other website-Orkut and then opened Gtalk. Orkut wasn't that interesting now. Even I stopped searching "Sinlge female Kolkata". But still, I already had many friends added and I started chatting with them.

My cell started ringing and I saw an unknown number. Unknown number always made my heart thump. This phenomenon started after my breakup. Every time I saw any unknown number, I thought she was calling from some other number. But consistently every time, I was left mistaken.

"Is this Rahul?" A husky female voice said as I picked the call. It was not Sonia's phone again.

"Speaking"

"Can I talk to you for a while? I'm Tania and I study in Xavier College. I came to know about you from some common friends"

"So"

"I mean I saw you singing today. You sang really well and I became your fan. Can we be friends?"

"Listen I'm...I...I have some work. Bye"

"One sec...one sec"

"Sorry. Bye" I said and cut the call.

"Who was it?" Yash asked.

"Some Tania was calling. She said she liked my singing today and wanted to have friendship with me."

"*Oye hoye*. Fans so early? We keep running after girls and girls are running after you!"

"I'm sure it's some stupid girl throwing pranks at us. Just ignore it" Yes I knew it was a prank. I had seen enough of these and I won't get trapped.

"Who knows? Something might happen. Talk to her. Give it a try"

"I know someone is fooling me. Even if it wasn't a prank, I don't want any relationship now. I'm happy single"

"Are you not over Sonia yet? Girl is coming after you herself and you are stopping her. Know what, iron cuts iron. Girls are the best antidote for the pains of other girls."

Meanwhile an SMS came, again from that unknown number or Tania's number "Pls talk to me once Rahul.pls.pls.pls"

My brain was getting all the more puzzled. What was happening? What should I do now? It was so complicated situation. So many things getting into it. What was the name...Tania...what if she really liked me? Should I...Na! I don't want to fall in other relation. And it was a prank after all.

I was in my thoughts and Yash gave her a missed call from my cell. And her call came the very next moment. Girls always sit with mobile in their hands.

"Talk to her. It isn't costing you anything. Do it man" Yash said.

"Hello" Tania said.

"Hi. I was busy in some work. So I cut the call. So what were you saying? "

"I was saying that I really liked your singing"

"Thanks. But from where did you get my number?"

"That I can not tell at this moment. I'll tell when we meet."

"You will have to tell this if you want me to talk to you"

"I told you na some common friend gave it. Name I can't tell now. But I'll tell later"

"Okay. But what did you like in me?"

"Your singing style. Your attitude. Everything. But why did you choose this specific song? It's my favourite"

"It's my favourite too and it's the favourite of most of the audience too plus our band played it well."

We talked till an hour about these things. It was strange that we can talk hours and hours to girls but with guys we try keeping the phone in a minute or two. And even this time the balance wasn't mine, so I was talking coolly to her without any sense of time.

"Do you have girlfriend?" She asked. How could she be so direct?

"No I don't have. What about you? Anyone special?"

"Not yet."

The chat continued till next half an hour. My ears and head started aching. I had to keep the phone now or else this girl would not stop.

"I'm feeling sleepy. Let's talk some other time" I said.

"Ok I'll call you tomorrow again. Thanks for talking to me"

"No sorry and thanks in friendship" I said lifting a famous bollywood dialogue.

"Okay bye." She said

"Bye"

"Take care"

"You too"

"Gud night"

"You too. Bye" I said and disconnected. Hadn't I disconnected she would had continued "sweet dreams" then "sleep well" and I don't know what else.

Union's Strength

Next morning Tania called again.

"Hello. How are you? How was your night?" She said. I never understand why girls ask these silly questions?

"It was okay. How was yours?" I also asked her as formality.

"Mine was nice too. By the way today also I'm coming to your college. Can we meet today? Please don't think otherwise. And please don't say no. Please."

"But"

"No ifs and buts. I know your classes are off and you are free. After all it's your fest going on" She was insisting so much to meet! How could I refuse?

"Okay then but when and where?"

"Outside OAT. 12:30 sharp" she said and disconnected.

Oh! I was going to meet a new girl today. I told this to Yash and he was very excited about this. But where was Viks? Yesterday also he didn't come till 12, I slept after that. And today also he was here at

11 am. Where was he? But his wet towel and undie were hanging. Did he bath again? Girls can change guys so much. Viks bathed two consecutive days, eighth wonder of the world(but again with the same dettol soap). But the girl, Rashmi, was not worth Viks. And I had to tell him. But he was busy in his own world. And. I had to talk about this face to face.

Meanwhile I started getting ready for today. It was feeling like the same day as Sonia's birthday when we met at Inox. I again wore my favourite blue shirt and sprayed half bottle deo and perfume. And I was thinking how would she look? Her voice was very cute, but what about her looks. Would it be equally cute?

Blunt 12:30, that is at 12:50 I was at the entrance of OAT. I called her up as I didn't recognise her but she recognised me.

"Hey. Where are you? I am at the gate of OAT."

"I waited fifteen minutes for you. Why were you so late? By the way I'm sitting in the A C Canteen. Come fast"

"But how will I recognise you"

"You just come na. Rest I'll see"

I marched to the A C Canteen. There were many couples and many girls sitting there as usual. I was trying to recognise Tania. I ran my over all the tables. Wherever I saw any beautiful girl I questioned myself "Is this Tania?" and when I saw even more beautiful then again thought "Is that Tania?"

"Rahul. Here." Someone shouted.

I went to the table from where a girl was waving her hand.

"Tania" I asked and she nodded. I stared at her face. She wasn't as fair as Sonia but her flawless skin was glowing. The problem in second relation is that we start comparing everything with our previous ones.

Her physique was not slim as Sonia but her figure was very good, almost near to perfect. Her hair was not long but short hair suited her face. And her lipstick smelt so tasty that I almost wanted to taste it. She was looking hot in red top, very hot and sexy.

"Hi. Should I get you coffee?" I asked Tania.

"I alrealy have. For you too" She already had bought two cups of coffee. Wow! Nice girl.

"Thanx. You look beautiful" I said.

"And you look good too" For the first time someone said this.

"So.."

"I saw you singing yesterday. You sang so well"

"Thanks" I said. We talked and talked for next one hour or so. It was strange that we were not feeling like strangers. As if this wasn't our first meeting. We were very much comfortable with each other.

"Hey Rahul. I am very much tensed. Please help me yaar. Actually we are participating in eastern choreography event but Prabir is ill. Could you please help us? Please do this favour for us"

"What? No no no. Please no."

"Please"

"No"

This looped six times after which I had to agree.

"When is your event?"

"Today 5 pm"

"What? Today? It's impossible. How will I do? Listen I don't know anything about dancing. I can't do. Sorry"

"You don't have to dance. Actually you don't have to do anything. You just have to hold a flag and that too for only thirty seconds or so.

And we have all the dresses prepared too. You don't have to worry about anything"

"Wardrobe Dresses?"

"Yes. The guy has to wear dhoti kurta"

"Nooo. I can't wear that" I protested.

"Please. For me. Just for thirty seconds"

I had to agree. We continued with our normal chat again gulping the coffee and munching pakora in A C Canteen. I found her very compatible with me. She was beautiful and intelligent too(rare combination).

At four pm, we went to change our dresses for the choreography event. We kept some time for little rehearsals. I was feeling very odd wearing dhoti kurta. But Tania was looking very dazzling in the ghaghra choli. She taught me what I had to do and we rehearsed it seven-eight times backstage.

Soon we were on the stage as it clocked five. Music started and she started dancing. She danced so well, her every step was right and her body movements were awesome. She was a trained dance for sure. Now it was my chance to come with the flag. I waved the flag which I had to do. I walked through the stage and she continued dancing, revolving or something. My job was over. Her dance ended after a few minutes. She called me subtly near her as her dance ended. She held my hand and bowed towards audience. I was a little late at understanding the situation so my bowing was not synchronous. And when she held my hand I almost got lost. Her hands were so soft, soapy. I smelled my hand to see that her hand actually had soap or what, but I got the smell of fantastic ladies perfume.

I was falling in love with her. Actually I was pushing myself to love her. She was the perfect girl for me. Beautiful, understanding, good natured, intelligent, very good dancer and my fan too. What else would I have asked for? She was the girl who could be my second girlfriend, my second love.

As we were getting down the stage, she again held my hand and said "Thanks for helping me."

"Mention not" I said while I was lost in thoughts of her soft hands. And still her hands were in my hands now, the cotton ball. I wished I could always hold her hand like this. Her hands were even softer than....Sonia...Sonia!!! Think of the devil and the devil was here. What was she doing here? She saw me holding Tania's hand. I jerked off Tania's hand.

"Hey. What happened? You look serious" She said watching my worried expression which came by default seeing Sonia. Shit! She saw me holding hand with Tania. Anyways what was wrong in that? Afterall I was not cheating. I liked Tania. And I wanted to start another relation with her, so there was nothing wrong in that. But why was I worried?

I grabbed Tania's hand again and she smiled. Sonia disappeared suddenly.

"Let's go and sit somewhere" Tania said. I decided construction would be a good place to hang out. But, Sonia was sitting there with her friends. No, I won't change my decision. I'd sit here only. Let Sonia and her friends see that I have a new girlfriend.

Sonia passed near us we glanced each other for a while but I turned my eyes away from her, towards Tania, the beautiful Tania, my girlfriend-to-be Tania. I'll love her.

Sonia again passed near us, this time with iced tea in her hand, her favourite. I avoided eye contact with her this time. Suddenly something showered on us – Sonia had spilt iced tea on us. Was it done deliberately?

"You go away from here. Why are you disturbing us?" I said scolding Sonia.

"Bloody girl spilt iced tea on us. Let's go and wash" I said to Tania.

"You knew that girl?" Tania asked. What to say now? That she was my ex-girlfriend.

"Yes. She is a college mate, very stupid silly girl"

We went to the tap near Aurobindo Bhavan. This tap had water for twenty hours, rest other taps were timed. Iced tea made her face glow more. She was looking gorgeous.

My cell started ringing. I took it from my pocket to see an unknown number. Unknown number again thumped my heart.

"Hello. Is this Rahul?" Voice came from the phone. It was her voice, Sonia's voice.

"Yes. Who is speaking?" I still enquired.

"Sonia." Bomb blasted in my heart. But I wasn't going to give up so easily.

"Who Sonia"

"You don't know me?"

"Give me some hint"

"You were in photography club right? And I met you there. Now you recognised?"

"Oh. You are speaking. Sonia Bose."

"Stop acting. It doesn't suit you"

"I'm not acting. I got a bit confused. Actually I know two-three Sonia's so.."

"Now this is overacting. By the way I called to say sorry for what I did."

"Yes you throw ice tea on us and say sorry. What do you expect from me? Tell frankly"

"Nothing. I just wanted to say sorry"

"No no. Say something. Scold me. You always like hurting me na. You just love it. Don't you?"

"Sorry"

"Sorry for what? Sorry is not your word. And anyways life is not to sit and regret. Life is to move on forgetting all the bad things"

"Am I bad? Have you forgotten me? Yes you did"

"When did I say that you're bad?"

"You were not recognising me, so you forgot me because I am bad"

"Who am I to comment whether Sonia Bose is good or bad. It's not my right. I am just an ordinary guy."

"That wasn't the answer to my question. Am I bad?"

"No you are right at your place. Everybody is right at his/her own place"

"I am saying again sorry for everything I did with you. I have forgotten everything"

"Everything means?"

"Everything means everything. Every fight between us. Every misunderstanding between us. Everything. I said na I have forgotten everything of the past"

Bomb number two blasted in my heart.

"Why? Suddenly? What has happened to you? Are you drunk? I

mean are you in your senses? You are Sonia Bose. You are saying sorry?? C'mon give me a break!!!"

"I am talking about past. Please don't misunderstand me. I know that I was very harsh on you that time. I realised my mistake and I am saying sorry for every moment now"

"Frankly tell me what do you think of me? Animal? Dumb ass? Or lame dog? Or even worse than that?"

"I think you are in a mood of fighting now, but I am not. We can talk later if you want"

"Mood? Later?"

"Sorry I don't want to hurt anyone now. Please don't misunderstand me. If you have to accept sorry than please accept it. It seems you are feeling odd, talking to me. Okay then I won't talk to you from now on. Same expectation from your side. Sorry again. Thanks for talking to me for one last time. Sorry if I disturbed you. Go and talk to the new girl. Bye"

"Bye" I said and disconnected the call. Again 10:01, one second factor. I was sure what I was doing. A bird in hand is better than two in the bush. I was following this saying. I was firm at my decision. Tania was surely with me and hopefully she would not betray me like Sonia did. But where was she? Actually I had travelled a lot while talking over mobile, old habits die hard.

I saw Viks moving hastily. I had to tell her about this thing and most importantly about Rashmi.

"Hey Viks"

"Hey Rahul what are you doing here?"

"Same question goes to you? And why did you came late last night and left so early today?"

"Actually I have some work regarding the fest. So I was a bit busy in that. Now also I have work."

"Okay. But listen I have to talk about something very important"

"Can we talk about it later? I have work now"

"No it's very urgent."

"Okay tell fast"

"That girl Rashmi is not good"

"How do you know her?"

"She is Sonia's friend. I met her in presidency college. She is a bitch. She has a long and dirty past of boyfriends"

"I know everything. She has told me already. Listen Boss! Physical past is very common these days and there is nothing like being second hand or anything. We're not cars or utensils afterall. And if your love is true, this thing won't come in your way. I know I'm not her first love. But being her last love is more important than being her first love. I mean, if you could love her so much intensely that she finally stays with you forever that is the ultimate pleasure"

"So you love her?" It was confirmed that he loved her, but still I asked. I was startled with all this? Whatever I had thought of telling Viks about Rashmi was rendered useless. How should I convince him that he was doing the wrong thing being with Rashmi. He had surely gone mad.

"Leave all this. Yash was telling that you got a new girlfriend Tania? Where is she?"

"She was here only, but don't know where she went. I have many other things to tell"

"Tell that later. I have to rush now. Bye" He said and ran.

Now where was Tania. She was not at the tap. She was not anywhere in the range of my eyes' vision. I tried her number, but it was busy. She was talking somewhere. I kept searching her in every nook and corner. Finally I found her sitting in the playground.

"Hey Tania" I shouted. Tania turned back and I noticed she was talking to Rashmi. Did she know Rashmi? How was that possible? It was a very weird day going for me. First meeting a new girl, then participating in choreo, then encounter with Sonia, Viks behaved strangely. What was going on?

Rashmi smiled seeing me and so did Tania. I sensed the smell of a plan. Oh! So it was all a plan, Rashmi gave my number to Tania and they were just making fun of me. I should have guessed that. It was a prank.

"So it was all a plan. Right?" I asked Tania. She smiled in return approving it.

"She gave my number to you?" I asked pointing towards Rashmi.

"No. She didn't" Tania said.

"Now please don't lie atleast. Even after all this. You all love hurting me right? I am a joker for you. You can anytime make fun of me"

"No I'm not lying and just chill. Take it easy yaar" Tania said.

Tania's words hurt a lot. It was feeling the same as when Sonia left me. I was felling agitated as well as dismal. Why did she do this to me?

It was the time of twilight, The sky was getting dark and so was my mood.

"Who gave you my number then? If Rashmi didn't give you" I asked angrily. I wanted to know who my hidden enemy was who gave Tania my number.

"Relax man. Why are you worrying so much? And what would

you do by knowing who gave your number. Just forget it. As if nothing had happened"

"Yes. I knew it means nothing to you to hurt somebody and break his heart. It's still fine but you will have to tell who gave my number? If you don't say by your own, I'll have to use other methods. Just tell me who gave you my number"

"I gave your number" It was Yash's voice.

"What? You gave my number? You wanted to hurt me? How could you do this?"

I was getting all the more confused. What was happening around me? What was going around here? Strange bizarre things were happening.

"Why Yash? Why did you do this?" I asked.

"It was for a reason" Rashmi said.

"You bloody. Keep your mouth shut" I scorned Rashmi. Meanwhile Viks also came.

"Viks you also knew about all this? You were also involved?" I asked Viks. His silence confirmed what he did not say.

"But why?" I asked again.

"We were checking how much do you love Sonia and you still love her or not" Rashmi said.

What? Again a bizarre thing. Suddenly I realised my calculation was wrong. The bird in the hand was Sonia and in the bush was Tania.

"And what did you find? That I don't love her anymore. Right?" And they had several instances to prove that. Tania herself being the biggest.

"When did I say this? I know you love me. I just wanted to say that I also love you" Sonia came from other side with her friends Monika and other two. What the hell was happening around me?

"Just forget it. Okay? Am I your puppet? Whenever you want you want you can kick me out of your life. And whenever you want you can come back. Enough is enough. I don't want any mercy"

"Why are you taking us wrong? I even said sorry. What else do you want? You know my degree is getting completed after two months" hearing this sent shiver through me. Her degree will get completed and she will leave the college. I can never see her after that. But it was good in some ways also.

"Congrats. Do your masters from a better college." I said as if I didn't care.

"Hey I'm really sorry. Tell me, how many times do you want to tell me sorry?" She said while walking towards me. I was determined not to get weak today.

"Why are you coming near me? I was the worst man on the earth for you"

"Who said this? I was keeping away from you because you are such a strong magnet. Had I talked to you even once I would have again been pulled by your magnetism. Let's not talk of that time. It was like a black spot. Please forgive me Rahul."

I kept quiet. I noticed, by this time Viks, Rashmi, Tania, Yash, Monika and Tania's two friends had encircled us. And Sonia and I were at the centre.

"What do you want now? Should I gift you a dog?" She said and giggled. So did everyone but me.

"You were so weird. I almost fell from the chair laughing when I heard this from my mom"

"I think you should write a mistake book like this one" Yash gave Sonia the MB or Mistake book, the seven paged book in which I wrote all my faults, all the mistakes which I had committed as well as my shortcomings.

"Read it aloud Sonia" Yash handed over it to Sonia.

"No. Don't" I said.

"Here we go. I'm short. I'm ugly. I'm fat. I'm arrogant. I'm short tempered. I'm immature.." I snatched the MB and tore it into pieces

"Whatever you all do. I don't, just don't want to be with her anymore" I announced firmly.

"But Rahul. Listen to us" Viks said.

"No no no. Infinite times no. Anyways why did you give Tania my number?" I asked Yash.

"I will tell you. But first listen to us" Yash replied.

"No" I said again.

I wanted to escape from there but I couldn't do. On one side there was stong Viks, fat Rashmi on the other, Yash and Tania on the third and Monika and all on the fourth. It was like I was playing a crossbreed of Kabaddi and ring-a-ring-a-roses. Everybody was surrounding me and was waiting for my breath to get over

"Give up man! Give up! See what is happening around you. We all are trying for your patch up. We all planned this for you. This is what you wanted Rahul. You know you are so lucky to get a friend like Viks who has girlfriend like Rashmi. How much they tried for you to make Sonia understand everything and clear the misunderstandings. And also thank College Unions without which Viks and Rashmi would have never met. And Tania who helped us in this drama. Thank God who made all this happen.

You are so lucky. Now don't spoil it." Yash lectured.

"But Tania was my fan. She liked my singing"

"She was not your fan. By the way our results were out. We lost again this time. And you sang awful" Yash said.

I broke down. My withstanding limit was crossed. I got senti in public. I started crying. I cried and they all laughed, but I noticed there was still one person who was in tears except me-Sonia.

Was it real? Or was I dreaming? I pinched myself and it pained. Yes it was real. Sonia was standing in front of me. I realised Union's strength. Hail Union.

I held her. I hugged her. And cried together. Everybody clapped. Yash and Viks whistled.

"Hey let's leave these freshly patched up couples alone. They must be having so much to talk" Rashmi said. They all left.

"Did you miss me? I missed you much. And truly speaking, I even couldn't delete your pics. I hid them in one corner of my lappy. When I was returning your school snaps, I scanned them before giving it to you. You must be getting many hiccups throughout the day coz I was missing you so much. But I never got even one hiccup. You never missed me or what?" I tossed.

"Shut Up" She said patting on my cheeks. She started glaring into my eyes, which soon got converted into kiss. I noticed a drop of tear rolling down her left cheek. It was looking awesome. I kissed over the tear. Girls look amazing with tears and I wish I could see her crying like this, with tears of happiness though.

"I love you." Sonia said. Her version of I love you had the feel of regrets.

"I love you too." My version of I love you meant it doesn't matter much.

At times 'I love you' seems to be the universal language of lovers in which they can express every emotion they want to. There are times when your love and emotions loses all control. I held her tightly in my arms and said "I'd never let you go. Never leave me again."

"Hey! I'm not a machine. Don't hold me so tightly. You're hurting me" She said.

"I'll crush you into my arms"

I saw her small face inside a hut of hairs. She was my girl. I loved those big eyes and dolphin earrings and her everything.

"What do you love in me?" I asked her.

"I love everything in you."

"What everything?"

"Okay I'll be a bit descriptive this time. I love your attitude. I love the way you talk. I love your silly jokes. I love your eyes, as I said earlier also, they appear very calm. You know in guys, the first thing I watch is eyes and yours are very innocent. Next I like the mole on your chin. And the way you love me. You are the best lover in this world. Is it okay now I can't lie more" She said laughing. I pulled her cheeks.

We talked and talked like never before. We were lost in ourselves as if we were the only two on this whole planet.

"Weather is good na?" She said and I got the signal for what I should do next. We went to our favourite cosy place.

Epilogue 1

Here was Sonia, back into my arms, for which I was striving for the last few months. It felt so good, like heaven, like you were drowning inside water and just got a breath of air when you were almost dying. It was like all my wish got fulfilled in a flash. Like my long cherished desire was completed. And that too at the most unexpected time. This is the paradox with life, you get the most when you expect the least.

And ya, the award function was held on the last day of the fest, we lost this time too. I knew it was all because of me. I understood that I was not a singer material and finally decided to quit singing. But Tania was bang on the first spot. Being a kathak expert she deserved that.

Time started running again and one year passed and I realised that girlfriends are not all-profit material. If there were benefits of getting back Sonia then there were consequences too. My alcohol and cigarette dosages were banned. And there was a regular check of my clothes and hankies whether they were clean or not; I felt as if I was in class eight. And my cellphone bill and monthly expenses were constantly alarming nani.

We decided to forget this kink of our life and never discussed this again ever. These past matters if ever discussed, gives only points to blame each other. And when fault is from the both side and both have admitted it, what's the point in repeating. Live life afresh and forget our sorrows. Life is too short, sometimes it takes too long to realise we're going the wrong way. All these things Sonia said. I couldn't give these philosophies.

I can never forget throughout my whole life what Viks did for me. He was also happy with Rashmi and his theory of not having girlfriend changed. This bastard always said girlfriends are evil and now...He started bathing too

Rashmi and my relation changed too. I took her so wrong, but she helped me even after all this.

Yash was recognised as a great guitarist and his band was performing great and he won many intercollege competitions. He was called to join a very famous band of Kolkata and who knows he might get very famous.

Another thing I realised was-both friends and love are integral part of our lives. One can't choose any of them solely or prefer one over another. Viks was great at equally carrying the two relationships.

But some things can never change I guess, and Sid and DUM DUM family are great examples. While Sid continued topping the class, Vishal kept talking of the same cartoons. Uncle kept eating my head. I wanted to put cellotape on his mouth and play tabla, taking his stomach as bigger and hairless skull as the smaller tabla.

It may sound very ironical but even after all this I loved this family. (I learnt irony from uncle). Who else would have done this much for me? Who would have made me feel as if I was a member of their family. They always loved me, but the way of expressing their love was a bit different. No one would have done this much, in a metro. Living in a metro teaches us many lessons and makes us realise soon that we are all alone. But the Dum Dum family never made me feel so and I loved them.

But After the battle of Dum Dum-II, things finally got changed a bit. Uncle appointed a new cook, Vishal's results were out and he finally got through the tough barrier of Tenth exams. In this happiness, one more TV was bought. I was happy because I got to watch TV and got good food. I went there every weekend now. Now aunty got more time for watching soaps as she didn't have to do the cooking and she was happy too. Everyone was happy.

Happy ending it was and all is well that ends well.

Epilogue 2

At 11:00 pm, my usual time to come online, I opened my gmail account again. I jumped to see a positive reply of publisher. They liked the manuscript and decided to publish it in a month. I was happy but more afraid, afraid because of the same what ifs: What if she never reads it? What if hates me more for this? What if she had forgotten me by now? What if she had another boyfriend? Will I get her back?

The book was released everywhere and also in the bookstore of my University and I couldn't resist my craving to watch my book in the shop. I went to the worldwide book store of JU and stood there at one corner. No one recognised me, so I could stand there easily unnoticed. Raj told me to gift the book to her, but I didn't do it. I was afraid she would think that these all were pretentions and show offs.

A week passed and my birthday came. Everyone wished me except her. And I can't tell how much it hurts when your loved ones don't wish you; it feels like the whole world has collapsed. I was as usual standing near the bookstore of JU. I saw her coming with her friends in the bookstore. I guessed she must have known about this book by now. I hid myself and peeped through the glass door. She lifted the book. Her friend also held one copy each. One of them said something pointing towards the book and then everyone smiled in reply and put the book where it was. No one bought it. I knew what they were doing-they were making a joke of me. I knew they must be saying "see the bastard hasn't still moved on. The loser can't find a new girl." The whole purpose of my writing the book was ruined. I would never get her back. My shoulders drooped and my spectacles got wet. This is what happens when your one year of labour gets in vain. You feel dejected and rejected. With what feelings and emotions I wrote every line every word -to make her happy, to make her realise my love. But this is my destiny. I can't get her. What will I do now? I can't do anything, a few months and she will leave the college. Her degree was about to complete in three months. I am a big loser. I lost it all, got nothing. I lost my time, wasted my labour and ultimately lost her. This was the end. I will never get her back. I went back to my room and wept and slept.

I got myself and my laptop off the sleep mode when it was 2 am. It was a 12 hour sleep straightaway. When you are disheartened you feel like sleeping the whole day. I opened my Orkut account and saw many birthday wishes again but there was nowhere her name. Then I logged in yahoo messenger. There were no offlines but it popped "you have got 2 mail messages". I opened my yahoo account, the first mail was of yahoo movie and I saw with my half-open eyes the sender of second message was......was... Sonia Bose. What??? Was I dreaming??? I widened my eyes and refreshed the page but it didn't change. In stories when you see these things you feel good but in reality you don't feel like believing it. Did she really mail me? Did she mail only to wish me? Or she had something more in her mind? Did she read the book? Was she angry with me? I'm always afraid of the unthought consequences of my deed. Did she mail just only to scold me about this crap? Or she mailed me to scoff at my work? With these questions in my mind I clicked on the mail to get the answers my question.

Hey Sonchu aka Mr writer (what should I call you now?),

What do you think of yourself? You will continue doing these silly things and I'll come back to you? Who do you think are you? What do you expect me to do? Read that book? And don't get angry at you, right? You won't stop running after me, would you? And what do you want to express by doing all this? That you love me? I already know that.

You are simply NUTS, MAD, PSYCHO, CRAZY, DAFT, MANIAC,(I'm getting short of words)......... I mean what is this? A whole book? For me? And you.......I never knew my chimpu was a writer. I mean you made those spelling mistakes.......how did u manage to write this much?

So this was all to impress me? To get me back? WoW!

If I tell you the reality, I also missed you, though I didn't show. I knew if I'd show my emotions in front of you I'd have become weak, so I had to be a little harsh towards you. But I'm confessing that I was hurt too, every time I hurt you. But I couldn't control myself after I read the book.

But I have serious complains about something. You didn't keep anything secret, you disclosed dharma bhrashta, our first kiss, my testimail. I can forgive you on that considering you were in a situation where you had to. But you fooled me with your experiments with emotions?? So you guys have everything planned?? Get ready for a big fight now!!! And what was this? You hid your mistakes and overprojected mine...This is not fair. You know what things I'm talking about.

I don't know if others would like the book or not but I loved it. How wouldn't I, it had parts of our real lives. But I didn't like the poison chapter. I would have never done a thing like that. I would rather have taken the poison myself and killed you if u did something like that. I mean guys should be strong. And I know my man is strong enough. And I saw you going to gym last month so you'll become stronger. What do you think, I too kept track of you all the time!

I thought we had completely different wavelengths and serious compatibility issues but I consider giving you a wild card entry for your work. Let's give it one more try because I have realized that maybe we are different culturally but we have intrinsic similarities. And we can always make adjustments, especially when you are ready too.

I want to say today what I was curbing inside me for the last one year- love you. I love very very very much. Be like this always. Love me like this always. Be with me always. Never leave me(and I also promise I'll never leave you) .fights n misunderstandings happen in every relationship....but neither of us should drag it n spoil the situation all the more...sorry I did.

But you know it's not my fault completely. But now when it's over let's not talk about it. Thankfully our love survived from both sides even such testing times.

My friends are also amused and they all want to meet you and want your autograph, the signed copy of your book. They were saying you are such a romantic hero. And we saw you standing near the bookshop, we were all laughing. Don't you have any other work than spying who is buying your book?? And that too on your birthday.......By The Way HAPPY BIRTHDAY. Where is my treat? Don't worry I have already bought a gift for you.

And wasn't it you who made my last number lifetime? When I was reading your book and came across such a thing, I doubted that....and when I checked my old SIM....It was still working even after one year....so I guessed that you did it.....But where the hell was your mobile? I kept trying your number the whole day, SMSed many times. Have you also changed your number?

My mom is impressed with you too. By the way I told everything to my mom about our relation and our hard times and about the book. And she wants to meet you too. She likes you even though you're too short. I want to marry you. Have two kids with the names we had decided.

I wanted to write more about this. I'm so much excited. But you know my mom! She can't let me sit in front of PC. She's calling for dinner. Meet you tomorrow in college at PCB. I'm gonna bunk all my classes tomorrow. Be there at 11 and don't be late. I have to talk so much. Love You. Take care

Mmmmmmmmmmmmmmmmmmmuuuuuuuuuuuaaaaaaaaaaaaahhhhhhhhhh

Warning : Don't disclose this mail or else I'll chew u raw.

I checked my mobile, there were 44 missed call and 20 SMSes from the same number, the old number of Sonia. I thought of calling her right then. But it was ~~2~~ two am and too late for calling her. I was regretting for keeping my cellphone in silent mode and for sleeping for twelve hours. Somebody exploded the tear gas bomb. I started thinking of the things to be said to her when I'd meet her after so many days. How much I missed her in the last one year. And there were many happenings which I wanted to talk to her. And I wanted to ask her if she got hiccups all the time as I remembered her all the time. Then I went to was my hanky and cut my nails. Damn happy I was. I was going to meet her just after a few hours....